A REALMSHIFT TRILOGY PREQUEL

THE

TABLET

S R Manssen

First published in New Zealand in 2023 by

Upside-down Books

ISBN 978-1-7385890-0-5 (pbk/ POD)

ISBN 978-1-7385890-1-2 (Epub)

ISBN 978-1-7385890-2-9 (Kindle)

ISBN 978-1-7385890-3-6 (PDF)

Upside-down Books

6 Rexford Heights

Tauranga 3112

New Zealand

www.srmanssen.com

Table of Contents

For my nephews Max and George

Other books by S R Manssen
The Realmshift Trilogy
Book One: Medar
Book Two: Tyrelia
Book Three: Golden City

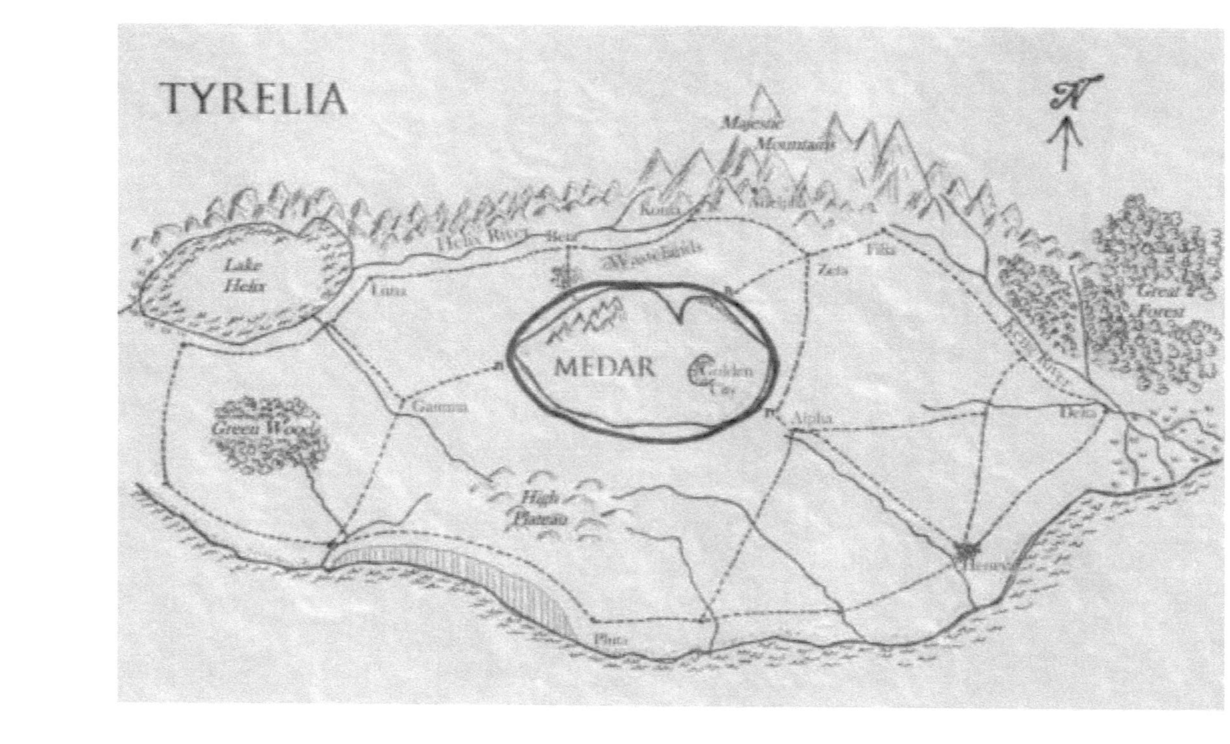

TYRELIA
N
Majestic Mountains
Great Forest
Lake Helix
Helix River
Bear
Woodlands
Zeta
Filis
Kona
Luna
MEDAR
Golden City
Gamma
Alpha
Delta
Green Wood
High Plateau
Pluto

Chapter 1 ————————ALERYCK

Aleryck twists his tongue, just so, and squints at the stones stacked on the boulder. He settles a pebble into his sling and spins it until it whirs. At the top of the arc, with practised timing, he releases the flap. The pebble flies through the air and smashes into his little pile of rocks, scattering them.

With a satisfied nod, he shoves the sling into his pocket. Now he needs to retrieve his pebbles. He flicks his thick black hair out of his eyes and, crouching slightly, hitches his homespun britches up around his skinny waist. He presses his bare toes into the rock for extra grip and prepares to jump ...

"Aleryck!"

He jerks his head up, loses his balance and slips off the boulder, arms flailing. He yelps as he slides feet-first into a tight space between two of the large rocks. He peers around. He can only just see over the tops. The tumble of boulders piled at the base of the cliff could be the scales of a giant lizard from this angle. "Who's there?"

Silence.

Aleryck puffs out his cheeks. It was just his imagination. Manoeuvring his legs under him in the crevice, he searches for finger holds in the boulders and heaves. *Aargh! That hurts.*

He leans back against one boulder, props his weak leg up and massages the withered muscles. It's not fair. His brothers—all seven of them—are perfectly fine. But him? No. He had to be born with this stupid twisted leg. Why him? Sure, he's still able to get around and stuff. But not without difficulty. It's why he's out here alone, leaping boulders while the goats graze, instead of back at the farm doing heavy chores like his brothers. He gives a quick grin. *Hmm. Perhaps having a bad leg has its perks after all.*

Taking a deep breath, he braces himself, pushes up on his good leg and slides onto the top of the boulder. *Made it.* He tugs his satchel around to his front, rolls onto his back and flops an arm over his eyes, shielding them from the midday sun.

"Aleryck." It's the same voice—if you can call it a voice. More like a whisper.

He bolts upright, scanning his surroundings. "Taran? Is that you?"

A cliff towers above him to his right. He's on a wide, rocky ledge that runs along the base of the cliff. To his left, the land drops steeply into a gorge where the Helix River chatters and dances its way southwards. The waterfall feeding the river cascades down the head of the valley behind him, and his goats graze the meadow that opens up beyond the rocks. He scans the opposite side of the valley. More rocks and another cliff, with snowy peaks visible in the distance—but no people.

The boulders surrounding him are devoid of movement. That leaves only the cliff face to his right. His gaze drifts over the surface. *Huh. What's that?* A wedge-shaped shadow directly opposite him is moving. Not a lot. But definitely moving—pulsing even. *Weird.*

Aleryck picks his way towards the shadow, using his hands to spider-walk from rock to rock. He'd rather not slip again, thank you very much. Now that he's closer, it's clear the shadow is caused by a section of rock jutting towards him, and it looks like ... *Yes!* His heart skips a beat. It's the entrance to a cave. He stands to get a better look. There must be a light source in there, flickering. *Maybe a fire?* Aleryck wrinkles his brow. It's the wrong colour for fire. More like moon or starlight. He glances at the sky. The sun hangs high in the blue expanse. Eyeing up the weird shadow once more, he takes a breath.

"Aleryck."

It's a whisper, but somehow loud in his head. And although it's inside his head, the voice is also coming from the cave. At the same time the light pulses, like it's connected to his name being spoken. His mouth drops open. *Gambolling goats!* He takes a step, then hesitates. Is it safe? Maybe he should go and get one of his brothers? He discards the idea as soon as it forms. Taran help him? Not likely. Taran doesn't like him, and the feeling is mutual. And the others ... well, they only do what Taran tells them to do.

He shuts his eyes, listening. A warm breeze ruffles his hair. A bird twitters and insects buzz. They're not alarmed, he reasons.

Alright then, he'll investigate it. But he won't go all the way in, just take a peek. *Yeah, that'll be safest.* He readies his sling as he creeps to the entrance, just in case.

As he steps into the opening, vibrations envelop him, beating in time with the light, like a heartbeat. They draw him in. He pauses while his eyes adjust. Wiping his clammy hands down his trousers, he shuffles down the narrow cave towards the faint, undulating glow. He'll just check that out, then leave. Rounding a sharp bend, he stops suddenly, transfixed. He throws a hand up, palm out, shielding his eyes.

In the middle of a cavern, suspended in mid-air, is the source of the pulsing white light. Suddenly bright, an object slowly rotates. It looks like ... a book?

"Aleryck."

He jumps, peering into the shadows that crowd at the fringes of the halo. "Who are you? Where are you? I can't see you."

"I am who I am."

"What do you mean?" Aleryck strains to see the owner of the voice.

"Some call me the Ancient. I am everywhere."

The Ancient! Aleryck's heard of the Ancient. Heck, everyone's heard of the Ancient. The Ancient is the benevolent ruler of Tyrelia. His Laws are good and kind, like 'Put others first' and 'Use your gifts for good'. The Ancient has always ruled Tyrelia, but he's never been seen. It's not like he rides around in a fancy carriage or makes speeches to the masses. Because he's not a person. He's the essence of Tyrelia. And now he's calling him—Aleryck!

Aleryck swallows hard. His heart hammers a crazy drumbeat. "Wha ... what do you want?"

"You."

"Me?" Aleryck squeaks. "What can I do? I'm just a fourteen-year-old with a crippled leg."

"I have a task for you, and you have the skills to complete it. Will you do it?"

Aleryck's mind races. Does the Ancient need someone to tend his goats? Surely there are other, stronger people who could do that. One of his brothers, for example. Or maybe he needs someone small and scrawny, who nobody will pay attention to? To do what, though? What could the Ancient possibly need Aleryck for?

"Skills? What skills?" he eventually manages.

The Ancient's words carry on the vibrations. They caress him gently, like his mother's hands when she smooths the hair off his forehead. "Your courage. Your perseverance. Your skill with lettering."

Aleryck blinks. Well, that's true. His handwriting is particularly good if he does say so himself. "Umm, alright. What do I need to do?"

"This." The object floating in the air pulses with a burst of light. "My tablet. My people are in need of my words. They are lost. I require someone willing to write my words onto this tablet so they can find me again."

That doesn't sound too hard. "Sure, I guess I could do that," Aleryck says.

"Once you've inscribed my words, the tablet will need to be taken into Medar."

Aleryck frowns. Medar? "You mean ... the Hole?" His voice catches on the word 'Hole'. That would be a lot more challenging. Leaving home. Travelling. His leg ...

The light changes to a softer tone. "Yes," says the Ancient. "You can do it, Aleryck. I will be with you."

In that moment, warmth flows through Aleryck, starting at the top of his head and travelling down to his feet. Like warm water being poured over him, but on the inside. Aleryck stands up straighter. Pushes his shoulders back. "I'll do it."

Can light smile? Apparently so. "Take the tablet," the Ancient instructs.

Aleryck reaches out a hand. The hairs on his arm stand upright as his fingers touch the object. *Cold. Huh?* He was expecting it to be warm. He grasps it with both hands and holds it reverently in front of him. It is made of some sort of glass but is not at all heavy. The smooth surface reflects the light. Which is strange, because he'd thought the tablet was the source of the light. He lifts his head. The pulsing glow is still hanging in the middle of the cave. "Now what?" he asks it.

The light flashes, and he stumbles a few steps backwards. His eyes widen. A new object is now rotating suspended in the glow. A stick?

"This is a special stylus for writing the words I will give you. Take it, Aleryck."

Clasping the tablet to his chest with one hand, he steps once more towards the light and takes the stick with the other. It is black, completely smooth, and pointed at both ends. One end sparkles in the light. Aleryck sucks in his breath. A gemstone!

"Are you ready, Aleryck?"

"What ... now?"

"Yes." The voice is quiet but firm.

He glances from the tablet to the stick. Licks his lips. "Ah, sure."

"The first words will need to be inscribed using the wooden end of the stylus, in the light of both a flame and full sun," instructs the Ancient.

"So, I need to make a fire ... outside?" Aleryck tucks the tablet in his satchel and makes his way back out of the cave. He blinks in the bright sunlight. The sun hasn't moved in the sky. It's as if no time has passed since he entered the cave. *Weird.* Right, now to find some wood to make that fire. *Oh!* A stack of sticks lies neatly against the cliff. If they'd been there when he entered the crevice, he didn't remember them.

He scoops them up and picks his way to a large, flat boulder nearby. First, he forms a pile of kindling with the twigs and scraps of bark. Then he criss-crosses the sticks over the kindling, ensuring plenty of air gaps. There, that should do it. He extracts the flint box from his satchel. Being a goatherd means spending days outdoors at a time, and he's known how to make a fire since he was five.

Before long, the fire is crackling. He pulls out the tablet and stylus and lays them carefully next to his fire. "I'm ready," he says.

The words form in his mind, sharp and clear.

> *Tyrelia! Land of gold*
> *A land so lovely to behold*
> *O, land of beauty, land of light*
> *Joyous refuge, pure delight*
> *Tyrelia! That land so fair*
> *Of meadows green and clean pure air*
> *Of stately trees in forests vast*
> *Of ancient rocks from ages past*

Positioning the tablet as close to the flames as he dares, so the light flickers across the surface, he picks up the stylus and, the tip of his tongue poking out, begins to write. As he makes the letter 'T' for 'Tyrelia', the stylus leaves a silvery trail. *Cool!* The letter looks like it's glowing. Aleryck smiles and continues writing. The stylus fits neatly in his hand, its weight and balance perfect for the task—like it was crafted especially for him. It probably was, he realises.

With enormous care, he finishes the two stanzas. He lays down the stylus, cricks his neck and rolls his shoulders, easing out the knots. The sun is sinking below the tops of the mountains and daylight is fading. Has he been writing that long?

He picks up the tablet, then freezes. The words have disappeared! His heart thuds. He drops to his knees and blows into the embers. The flames leap as he holds the tablet close to them.

Faint at first, then bright, the silvery words appear on the surface. Testing a theory, he turns his back to the flames, and the words fade. Then he once more holds the tablet close to the flames and the writing reappears. He sighs in relief and closes his eyes, clutching the tablet to his chest. So, the tablet is magical, and the words appear in flamelight. That's so cool. He'll check them tomorrow morning in sunlight, too, just to be sure.

He scrambles to his feet and slips the tablet and stylus into his satchel. He hesitates, then lifts his face to the sky. "Thank you, Ancient," he says. "I've got to go home now, but I'll come back tomorrow, I promise."

Calling to the goats, he jogs home as fast as he can.

Chapter 2

Taran scoops a handful of water from the trough and splashes it onto his face, rubbing it through his hair. Ah, that feels better. They've worked hard today, he and four of his brothers, planting out the last of the new grape vines on the steep rocky hills of their family land. They'd been dripping by the end of the day, despite it being only early spring.

His parents are lucky to have so many strong sons. Except for Aleryck, of course—what a waste of space that one is! Not only is he a lazy little sod who keeps on using his bad leg as an excuse not to do any real work, but he's also such a snitch. Yet Ma can't see it and always takes Aleryck's side. Just thinking about Aleryck makes Taran grind his teeth.

Even though the farm work is physically demanding, he likes it. It keeps him strong, and he knows the girls like a strong man. He quite fancies his chances with the local village beauties. There aren't many to choose from so, being eighteen and his brothers each about a year apart—except for the youngest, the twins, Kepler and Seb—there's a bit of competition. Thankfully, his two older brothers are already married, and he knows that with his green eyes and dark hair, he has a good chance of snagging one of the prettier ones. That Dessa, for example. He feels the strength in his firm body and can't help but flex a bicep.

"Hey! Taran's preening again," Baydar crows. Just a year younger than Taran, Baydar is Taran's closest ally. But he can also be his biggest rival.

"Am not," he retorts, flicking water onto Baydar. *That should shut him up.*

Baydar splutters, whipping his head from side to side. Drops of water fly in all directions. "Right, game on!" he says. Plunging both hands into the water, Baydar splashes Taran.

Taran narrows his eyes at Baydar. *I'll teach him.* "I mean it. Don't splash me." He scoops a palmful of water into Baydar's face, ending with a slap on his brother's cheek. Not a gentle slap, either.

"Water fight!" shouts Noor. At sixteen, he's just gone through a massive growth spurt, and is all bony elbows and knobbly knees. He's at that uncoordinated stage, and in his excitement manages to trip over his own feet, sending the twins, Kepler and Seb sprawling. He's oblivious that this is not a play-fight for Taran.

Luckily, the twins are not only rather plump, but they're also up for a good bit of rough and tumble. They scramble to their feet and join in.

Taran steps back, his arms folded across his chest, watching his brothers with disdain. *Such children.* Soon, the four boys are soaked, the dirt has turned to mud underfoot, and there's no water left in the trough.

"Taran! What is the meaning of this?" His ma's voice cuts through the racket, stopping him in his tracks. He spins to face her, swiping the damp hair out of his eyes. She stands on the doorstep, hands on hips, and has that 'don't mess with me' look on her face.

What? I wasn't even part of it. But Ma always blames me, just because I'm the eldest now. "Sorry, Ma." He drops his head to give him time to hide his anger and compose his expression into one of contrition. He senses his brothers shuffling in behind him. He can't blame any of them in front of Ma. He'll have to deal with Baydar later when he can get him alone. The thought cheers him up. He picks up the bucket sitting beside the trough and smiles at Ma. "I'll go get more water."

Ma nods. "Thank you. The rest of you—go wipe that mud off your feet then come inside and get changed before dinner."

As he rounds the corner towards the well, Taran almost bumps into Aleryck, who is hop-skipping at pace towards him. "Whoa, little brother, why the hurry?"

Aleryck's eyes are bright, his cheeks flushed. "Hey, Taran," he says, breathless. "I've got some news."

Taran tilts his head, eyes calculating. "Is that so?" *Now what has the little sneak been up to?* "Did you meet a girl today?" he sneers.

Aleryck blushes bright red. "No! I ... I've got something to show Ma." His hand strays to his satchel.

Taran lifts an eyebrow. "Well, before you do, make yourself useful and fill up the trough." He thrusts the bucket into Aleryck's arms and turns on his heel. *Nice work getting out of that chore, Taran.* He saunters off.

∞∞∞∞∞∞

Taran hides a smirk as Aleryck limps into the kitchen. Everyone else is already seated at their long table, which is laden with food. Their pa's absent: he's away in Konia tending to their casks of maturing wine with his elder brothers. He's often away for weeks at a time. But because they've been planting, his aunt Naomi—Ma's sister—is staying with them to help, along with his cousin Jazmyne.

"So, what is it you wanted to show us, Aleryck?" Taran asks. Seven heads swivel towards Aleryck.

Aleryck colours. "What? Now?"

"Sure."

Aleryck slips his hand into his satchel. Reverently, he pulls out a block of glass.

Taran leaps up, crosses to Aleryck in two strides, and snatches it out of Aleryck's hands. "Ooh, some glass. This is so *amazing*."

Aleryck hobbles over to him and attempts to grab it. "Give it back, Taran. It *is* amazing. The Ancient gave it to me."

Taran snorts. *Really?* He brings it closer to his eyes. "Why?"

Aleryck reaches for the tablet again, so Taran holds it higher. "Because," Aleryck pants, "I'm inscribing it with special words that the Ancient has given me."

Taran inspects it again. "Oh. When will you start?"

"I have started." Aleryck scowls.

Taran raises an eyebrow. "Ah, I hate to say this, but you haven't."

Baydar jumps up. "Maybe your eyesight isn't so good, brother." He snatches the tablet out of Taran's grasp. Screwing up his eyes he peers at the piece of glass. Shakes his head. "Nope, nothing wrong with your eyesight. There's nothing here."

Aleryck leaps at Baydar. "I *have* written on it. But it's magic. You can't see it in this light."

Baydar's eyes go wide. "Oho, magic is it?" He waggles the tablet out of reach of Aleryck's flailing hands. "Look, Taran, a magical piece of glass!"

"Let me see." Noor joins the brothers.

Baydar tosses it to Noor. "Catch!"

Noor nearly drops it. "Got it," he gasps, clasping it to his stomach. It's his turn to inspect the tablet. "Doesn't look magical to me, Aleryck." He shrugs.

Aleryck spins to Noor with clenched fists. "But it is," he says. "I can't help it if the Ancient chose me and not any of you. Give it back." He lunges at Noor.

Noor steps back, raises his arm and tosses the tablet to Taran. "Catch!" he yells.

So, the Ancient chose Aleryck, did he? Taran scowls. *What a load of horse dung.* As the object tumbles towards him, he shoves his hands in his pockets and steps sideways. It crashes onto the flagstones beside him and smashes into a million pieces.

"No!" Aleryck screams. He drops to his knees, arms outstretched, sweeping the shards of glass towards him. Sobbing, he tries to press them back together.

Taran catches his mother's scowl. *Better look contrite.* "Hey, I'm sorry little brother. But it was just a piece of glass ..." He places a hand on Aleryck's bony shoulder.

Aleryck shrugs it off and wipes at his eyes with the back of his hand, before continuing to scrape the fragments of glass together. His hands are bleeding.

"Aleryck, love," Ma says. She swoops down on Aleryck, glaring daggers at Taran. "Leave that now. We'll clean it up later. Let's get your cuts seen to." She gently picks shards of glass out of his palms, before easing him upright. "Come now." She leads him away.

Taran reaches out a hand as Aleryck passes, but lets it fall to his side. *Honestly, the kid's so worked up about a dumb piece of glass. And fancy claiming the Ancient gave it to him! The little snot is so up himself.* He shakes his head. If the Ancient were going to choose any of them, he'd choose Taran, not a cripple. Anyone could see that.

He sighs and gets the broom. He'll have to pretend to make it up to Aleryck. Maybe get him a nice notebook from Konia next time he goes there. The kid likes to scribble.

Yeah, that'll do the trick.

Chapter 3---------SECOND CHANCE

There is nothing for it. He's going to have to face the Ancient sooner or later, so it may as well be now. Aleryck might be scrawny, and Taran might think of him as a 'cripple', but he isn't a coward.

Balanced on a boulder in front of the cave entrance, he calls, "Ancient?" His voice catches, echoing off the cliffs.

No response.

He shades his eyes with his forearm, scanning his surroundings for any sign, but he should've known the Ancient wouldn't be here. Aleryck had been given a chance to do something special—great even. And he'd blown it. He blinks away the threatening tears, sniffing.

Suddenly, light pulses from the shadows in the cliff face. His heart leaps. *The Ancient is still here!* Aleryck squares his shoulders and, taking a deep breath, limps into the cave entrance.

Once again, he is enveloped by a comforting presence. The pulsing light guides him deeper into the cave towards the chamber. He pauses, trembling, before stepping around the corner into the brightness. He gasps.

There, suspended in the middle of the cave, is another glowing tablet.

"Oh," he exclaims. *How did he know?*

"I see everything, Aleryck," the Ancient says in his mind. "I know how the tablet was smashed. Just as I know that, in the future, my people will need my words. So, Aleryck, I ask you again: Will you scribe my words?"

Aleryck doesn't even need to think about it. "Yes," he says. "Of course, I will." He reaches out and takes the tablet, the hairs on his arm prickling. He hugs it to his chest. "I'll go make the fire."

He hurries outside and sets to his task. Before long, a fire is crackling merrily on the same rock as yesterday, and Aleryck is crouched over it, inscribing the tablet with the special stylus, frowning in concentration.

After an hour he is done. He puts down the stylus, rolls his head and stretches his fingers and arms, massaging out the cramps. "Now what?" he asks.

"I will need you to return tonight. The next stanza needs to be inscribed by moonlight. But first, there is something else to be done."

Aleryck nods. "I'll do it."

"Use the diamond tip to etch these numbers at the bottom: *5–63–92–99.*"

"Do I need to stoke up my fire?"

"No, the numbers will always be visible."

"Oh. Why? What are they for?"

"That will be revealed tomorrow."

Aleryck frowns. Alright then, he could be patient. Crouching once more, he carefully etches the numbers along the bottom of the block of glass. *There, done.*

Aleryck stands up and is about to tuck the tablet away in his satchel when he pauses. "I think I'll leave this tablet here, in the cave. You know, for safe keeping," he says.

The Ancient doesn't reply, but Aleryck feels like he agrees.

Aleryck hobbles back down the passageway and looks around the cave. He spies something crumpled against the wall and picks it up, rubbing it between finger and thumb. A piece of soft leather—goatskin perhaps? He doesn't recall seeing that there before but, then again, stuff seems to appear just when it's needed in this place. He wraps the leather around the tablet and stylus and nestles them into a corner.

Straightening, he hitches up his trousers. "I'll see you tonight then," he says to the cave.

The light pulses in reply.

∞∞∞∞∞∞

Aleryck chases the potatoes around his plate with his fork, daydreaming about what the Ancient might need him to write next.

"Aleryck, honey, aren't you hungry?" Ma asks from the other end of the table.

He jerks his head up in time to catch her shooting a look at Taran, her lips pursed.

Taran lifts a shoulder, then half-turns to Aleryck. "Hey, I'm going into Konia tomorrow. Do you want to come with?"

Aleryck's heart thumps. *No!* The Ancient will need him to inscribe more verses on the tablet. But he can't possibly tell Taran that—he'll just scoff at him again. Or worse, smash the new tablet. He shakes his head, trying to figure out what he can say, discarding thoughts as soon as they form.

Taran huffs and hunches over his empty plate. "Told you he wouldn't want to come with me," he mumbles.

His ma pats Taran's forearm. "At least you tried," she says.

Whew. That was close. "May I be excused?" Aleryck asks, taking advantage of the moment.

"Of course, honey," Ma says. "Noor, will you clear the plates, please?"

Aleryck slips from his chair. How's he going to do this? He shares a room with Seb and Kepler, so they will definitely notice if he leaves now. Unless he stuffs his pillow under his blankets. Would that fool them? Maybe. Maybe not. *Not worth the risk.* That's settled then. He'll wait until they're asleep before sneaking out.

∞∞∞∞∞∞

Aleryck strains his ears. His brothers' breaths are slow and even. He slides out from under the covers, hesitates, then shoves his pillow under the blanket just in case. He creeps across to the door. The latch clicks as he lifts it. The sound is horrendously loud in the still night. Seb snores once, then moans as he rolls over. Aleryck freezes, his heart hammering. Seb's breathing returns to a steady rhythm and Aleryck exhales. He slips out of the bedroom, down the hallway and through the front door. Sinking onto the front step, he fumbles with his shoes. He sets off in the direction of the cliffs.

As he hobbles past the goat pen, one of the goats bleats. Aleryck jumps with fright and stumbles against the railing. Another goat stirs and bleats. *By the Ancient! They'll wake the family.* "Shh," he whispers, reaching over the fence and stroking the goat's nose. "Hush, hush, now." But the goats won't settle down. Perhaps some hay will help? He diverts to the haybarn to collect some.

Even though one end of the building is unobstructed by doors, the interior is dark, so Aleryck shuffles inside. He's only a few steps in when his foot catches on something blocking his path, and he stumbles forwards with a cry, arms outstretched. His fall is broken by the lumpy object he tripped on.

"Ouch, get off me," it yells.

Taran. He's fallen on Taran. What in Tyrelia is Taran doing sleeping in the haybarn?

Taran shoves Aleryck off him and sits up.

Then a second person sits up. "Who is it, Taran?" It's a girl's voice.

"Jazmyne?" Aleryck squeaks, blinking hard. "What are you doing here?"

Taran scrambles to his feet and hauls Aleryck up by the front of his tunic. Taran's face looms so close, their noses almost touch as he snarls, "Don't you dare tell Ma."

Aleryck can't believe his luck. He takes a deep breath and screams at the top of his lungs, "MAAAAA! Help, help! My leg." Taran drops him like a hot coal and Aleryck scuttles out of reach before racing out of the barn to the house.

He hears Taran chasing him, but it's too late. Ma is running towards him with a lamp, and Aleryck throws himself into her arms. He sobs for good measure.

"What is it Aleryck, love? What's wrong?" Ma holds him tight. Then she stiffens and her tone changes. "Taran? Jazmyne? What is going on here? I think you have some explaining to do. Inside, now!" She points to the open door, where three of his brothers and Aunt Naomi are all gathered, gaping.

She turns, holding Aleryck tight and helps him indoors. "Ouch!" he cries, bending to rub his leg ... and to hide his smile.

∞∞∞∞∞∞

It's the following night. Aleryck has managed to sneak out of the house again without waking anyone. Thankfully this time there are no bleating goats or tripping-over-Taran incidents to slow him down. Taran is in a whole lot of trouble now—Ma has grounded him for a month! Aleryck doesn't feel bad about it though. Serves Taran right for smashing his tablet. He just hopes the Ancient isn't mad at him for not showing up last night.

The moon is full and bright, making it easy to pick his way across the boulders to the cave entrance. He rounds the corner and walks towards the pulsing light emanating from the cave. "Hello? I'm here," he calls. "Sorry I couldn't make it yesterday ..." He holds his breath, straining his ears.

After several heartbeats, the Ancient says, "Welcome, Aleryck. Let us continue."

Aleryck exhales. He hurries to the bundle and extracts the tablet and stylus. Exiting the cave once more, he seats himself on the ground and places the tablet on a large, flat boulder. "Alright, I'm ready."

"Make sure the moonlight is shining fully on the surface before inscribing these words:

> *Majestic mountains, white with snow*
> *Their crystal tears to rivers flow*
> *Splashing sparkles dance up high*
> *Painting rainbows in the sky*
> *Swathes of splendid floral hues*
> *The land with colour do imbue*
> *The golden sun smiles down from high*
> *As he marches 'cross the sky"*

Aleryck sucks in his cheeks as he hears the words. "Beautiful," he sighs as he begins writing.

The moonlight floods the tablet, and the letters shine bright silver as he forms them. Whenever he falters and can't remember the next word, the Ancient sets them in his mind. Biting his lip in concentration, Aleryck continues his task. Finally, he completes the last word. "Finished," he announces, setting down the stylus.

"Good work, Aleryck," the Ancient says. "Now, do you want to know what the numbers mean?"

Aleryck nods. "Yes please."

The Ancient's response forms in his mind. "The poem I am giving you is about Tyrelia. There will come a time when all memory of this beautiful land will be lost. The poem on this tablet will provide the clues as to how to find the way back to Tyrelia."

Aleryck can't believe there will ever be a time when people won't remember Tyrelia, but who is he to question the Ancient?

"Various substances will cause different verses to appear on the tablet. As you have guessed, the verse you wrote yesterday will appear when exposed to sun or flamelight. Tonight's verse will appear in moonlight."

Aleryck smiles. He had worked that out correctly.

"But how will the person who discovers the tablet know which substance to expose the tablet to?" the Ancient asks.

Yes. How?

"That's where the numbers come in. There are forty-six words in the first two stanzas I asked you to scribe, but the first number you etched is fifty. So, if you keep counting into the third stanza that you wrote tonight, the fiftieth word is—"

"Snow!" Aleryck exclaims.

"That's right. And the sixty-third word is 'rainbows.'"

"Cool," Aleryck says, scrambling to his feet. Then he stills as he bends to pick up the tablet. "Uh, but then I'll have to get to the snow to write that clue?"

"Yes," the Ancient confirms. "But remember, I will help you. It's time for you to go now, Aleryck. Meet me tomorrow at the headwaters of the Helix River."

Aleryck nods in understanding. He carefully wraps the tablet and stylus in the goatskin and hides them in the cave. Then he practically floats home, as if on a cloud. He still can't believe the Ancient has chosen *him* for this task.

He really is so much more important than his brothers.

Chapter 4‒‒‒‒‒‒‒‒SNOW AND RAINBOWS

It's mid-morning by the time he gets to the headwaters of the Helix. First, he had to swing by the cave to collect the tablet. Then he had to settle the goats grazing nearby.

Now, he's in the narrow valley where the snow-fed Helix River tumbles from a cliff towering above him, before flowing between clumps of moss and boulders at his feet. Tiny droplets of spray sparkle in the sunlight, and bright green ferns cling to the rocky face, thriving in the damp environment. But it's cold. Thin crusts of ice have formed over some of the mossy rocks and a chill wind nips at his ears.

Aleryck wraps his arms around himself and shivers. "Hello," he calls. "I'm here."

"Aleryck," the Ancient says. "How are you, my son?"

"Cold ... but ready," he hastens to add, in case the Ancient thinks he's making excuses.

"First, you'll need to get to the snow."

Aleryck cranes his neck, squinting up at the waterfall, where icicles cling to the tip of each rocky protrusion. "Up there?" he asks, his voice full of doubt.

"Yes. Go to the large fern."

It's at the base of the waterfall, off to the right. Aleryck scrambles over to it. The plant is massive—twice as tall as him. "Now what?" he asks.

"Look behind it," the Ancient instructs.

Aleryck edges his way around the fern and, using both hands, pulls the fronds away from the rock behind. "Wow! There's stairs here," he exclaims.

He squeezes behind the green canopy. The staircase winds its way upwards, concealed by rocks. Adjusting his satchel strap, he starts climbing. Sheltered from the biting wind and, to an extent, the fine spray, it's considerably warmer here. Almost like being inside a chimney. It's so far to the top, it seems to take forever before he finally emerges onto a thin layer of snow coating the ground. *Perfect*. The Ancient shares the words into his mind:

Who alone has claim to rule
Tyrelia, beyond the Wall
Tyrelia! O, land of gold
O, land so lovely to behold

"Is that all?" Aleryck asks.

"Would you prefer a longer verse so you can spend more time in this snow?"

"No, thanks." Hiding a smile, Aleryck shakes his head and, dropping to his knees, pulls out the tablet and stylus. He scoops up a handful of snow and smears it across the surface of the tablet. "Like this?" he asks.

"Yes. Brush snow over the surface between each line."

Aleryck does as he is told. The short verse doesn't take long to pen but, even so, he is shivering by the time he is done. Just to make certain he's done it right, he lets the words fade before rubbing snow over the surface once more. He sighs with relief when the silvery writing reappears.

"Well done, Aleryck. Now for the next one. Back down the stairs."

Dusting snow off his palms and knees, Aleryck rubs his hands together before making his way back down the staircase. Down is always harder, due to his leg. It makes him nervous—ever since his leg gave way and he fell down a flight of stairs when he was younger. At least it's warmer here, though. His knees wobble and he clutches the rocks for support. "Ouch," he yelps when he scrapes a knuckle. He sucks at the graze. Squeezing back past the giant fern, he emerges at the base of the waterfall.

"Look at the waterfall. What do you see?"

I've just looked at it. But he turns as directed. "Uh, water," he says, a little too sarcastically.

"Who are you talking to?" a sneering voice asks from behind him.

Aleryck spins, his heart thumping. "Taran? What are you doing here?"

Taran crosses his arms. "I asked you first," he says.

"You're not allowed to be here," Aleryck counters. "I'll tell Ma."

Taran raises an eyebrow and slowly scans the narrow valley they're in. "I'd like to see you try to beat me home."

Aleryck's shoulders slump. What should he do? An idea pops into his head. It might work. "You wanna see something cool?"

Taran's lip curls, like Aleryck couldn't possibly know anything 'cool'. "Sure," he says.

"It's behind that fern," Aleryck says, pointing. He hobbles over to it and pulls back the fronds. "See?"

Taran saunters to him and peers over Aleryck's shoulder. "Huh," he says, "that is cool." He squeezes around the fern and, standing on the bottom step, cranes his neck. "Where does it go?" he asks, his voice echoing slightly around the void.

"Just up to the top. Great view from up there. And there's snow," Aleryck adds.

"You climbed up there?"

No need to sound so incredulous, Taran. "Yes, I did."

"What for?"

None of your business. "Just exploring," he lies.

"I'm going to check it out. See ya." Taran disappears up the staircase.

That suits Aleryck. "Yeah, I'm going to head back to the goats, now," he calls to Taran. This is the chance he was hoping for. He directs his thoughts to the Ancient. "I'll come back when I can, Ancient."

"I'll be waiting," the Ancient speaks into his mind.

Aleryck hurries back to the cave. Just as he reaches it, he hears Taran approaching. He scrambles inside and crouches down, panting hard.

"Aleryck? Where are you?"

He daren't move—Taran might hear him. He tries to control his breathing.

"Aleryck! I know you're here somewhere." Taran's feet slap as he leaps from boulder to boulder, then he makes a noise of disgust. "Play your stupid hiding game then. I'm going home."

Aleryck closes his eyes, resting his head against the rocky wall, and counts slowly to a hundred. When he's done, he strains his ears. Nothing. He crawls to the exit and slowly, slowly peers out. Taran is nowhere in sight. He breathes a sigh of relief.

Getting to his feet, he shuffles out of the crevice and returns to the waterfall. "Ancient?" he calls.

"Aleryck. Come, we have work to do. Look at the spray from the waterfall. What do you see?"

At that moment, a shaft of sunlight stabs into the valley like a pointing finger. Aleryck gasps. "A rainbow!"

"Here's your next verse:

> *As flaming sunset turns to night*
> *Stars and moon cast silver light*
> *On all who choose to live lives free*
> *From the Master's tyranny*
> *He has no claim to any throne*

He long ago was overthrown
By the Ancient, true and just
In whom all living things can trust"

Aleryck positions the tablet where the rainbow light touches the ground and sets to inscribing the words.

It's uncomfortable, squatting. His bad leg is going numb. He stands and stretches, hobbling around and swinging his arms to get some circulation going. Even though the droplets of spray from the waterfall are tiny, his tunic and breeches are wet through. If it weren't for that sunlight so conveniently penetrating this valley, he'd be a block of ice by now.

Finally, he's done. Beaming, he holds the tablet into the rainbow light and reads the verses again. "So, last night the moonlight verses had 'rainbows' as the sixty-third word. How many more words came after that?" he asks, frowning, trying to remember.

The Ancient places the words in his thoughts:

Painting rainbows in the sky
Swathes of splendid floral hues
The land with colour do imbue
The golden sun smiles down from high
As he marches 'cross the sky

"It's another twenty-seven words after the word 'rainbows'. Which makes—"

Aleryck counts in his head. "Ninety!" he blurts.

"Yes."

Aleryck checks the tablet. "The next number is ninety-two, which is 'flaming'. That means the flames I did on the first day, right?"

"That's right," the Ancient confirms.

"And then ..." Aleryck counts the words revealed by the rainbow light. "...'moon' is the ninety-ninth word. I'm done!" he crows.

"Not quite," the Ancient says.

"Whaddaya mean, *'not quite'?*"

"Well, the tablet has two sets of poems. One set that displays in Medar, and one in Tyrelia."

"Oh." The elation he momentarily felt drains out of him like grain through a hole in a sack. "So, I'm only half-way done?"

"No, there are only three more substances to go. And the next one is Helix water, which you can do now."

The grain stops draining. Only two more substances after this? He lifts his chin. "Alright, what are the next words?"

> *Fresh clean air, sparkling waters*
> *Quench your thirst, sons and daughters*
> *Head to the place with sulphurous steam*
> *To free Medar from the Master's schemes*

Aleryck crouches once more, this time at the edge of the stream. He dips the tablet into the water before writing the words. After each line, he wets the tablet again.

"Wow," he breathes, when done. "*To free Medar from the Master's schemes,*" he quotes. "It sounds so ... big."

"Nonetheless," says the Ancient, "you can do it. You need to have faith in yourself, as I have faith in you."

Aleryck wraps the goatskin around the tablet. "I'd better get back to the goats now. What are the last two substances?"

"One is honey," says the Ancient.

Aleryck frowns. He doesn't remember writing the word 'honey'.

"The other is 'sulphurous steam.'"

What? That sounds dangerous. "I know where to get some honey." There's some in the pantry at home. "But where would I go for the 'sulphurous steam'?"

"To the Wastelands. Aleryck, tomorrow we start the journey to Medar. Are you ready?"

The Wastelands? Aleryck gulps, then squares his shoulders. He's not sure how he'll manage it, but he's willing to try if that's what the Ancient wants.

Chapter 5--------A SMEAR OF HONEY

Taran whistles as he saunters into the kitchen. Aleryck is seated at the table, crouched over something, with Ma at his side. Taran narrows his eyes. "Whatya doing?" he asks.

Aleryck's head whips around, shock in his eyes, and he hunches protectively over whatever it is he's got. "Taran," he croaks.

"That's my name; don't wear it out." Taran grins at his own wit.

Ma places a gentle hand on Aleryck's shoulder as she swivels to face Taran. "Aleryck has been given a very important task by the Ancient," she says.

Not that again. "Uh, really?" he manages.

"Yes," Ma says. She shifts so that Taran can see what they are doing.

Taran gapes. That smashed up block of glass is sitting there on the table, perfectly whole again! Although, admittedly, it's not as clean as it was before. It's covered in a film of yellow goo. His eyes flick to the clay jar next to Aleryck's elbow. Honey. The goo is honey. "How ...? What ...?"

Aleryck glowers at him over his shoulder. "Yeah, that's right, Taran," he says, lifting his chin. "The Ancient gave me another tablet."

Ma adds, "And you, Taran, are going to help him to accomplish his task."

Taran gestures at the table. "You need me to help smear honey on it?" he asks, his lip curling.

Ma tsks. She stands and wags a finger. "If that's what were needed then, yes, I would expect you to do it. But it's not." She steps towards him. Even though he towers over her, Taran takes a step backwards. "Aleryck needs to go to the Wastelands. You are going to accompany him." She stabs her finger at him as she says this.

"The Wastelands? Why there?"

Aleryck turns to face him, squaring his shoulders. "I've been given a special task to write a message on this tablet that is going to save the world one day. The words are activated by different substances. I need to write the words with this special stylus with each substance. I've done them all except *sulphurous steam*. Which is in the Wastelands."

Special task. Special stylus. It makes Taran's blood boil. He clenches his fists. But he can see there's no changing Ma's mind. Alright then, he'll go. Anything would be better than being grounded—even going to the Wastelands. Might give him a chance to teach mister 'I'm so special' a lesson along the way. Take him down a peg or two. *Yeah*. He might need some help with that, though.

He smiles at Ma, raising his arms, palms out in surrender. "Of course, I'll go," he says in his most soothing voice. "It'll be quite a journey, though. Maybe all of us brothers should go. You know, safety in numbers and all that."

She smiles, looking pleased. "I was going to suggest that. I knew I could rely on you to protect Aleryck from the snakes and those wild people that live there—you know, those drifters and bandits." She nods her head. "That's settled then. You'll get packed and set off in the morning."

"But Ma," Aleryck protests, "How will you manage the goats and everything?"

"Oh, with the planting finished, Naomi and Jazmyne here, and your pa due home any day, we'll only be alone for two days at the most. Two days of peace and quiet! I can hardly wait." She drops a kiss onto Aleryck's head before disappearing into the pantry.

From the muffled bangs and thumps that follow, Taran guesses that she's sorting out supplies for their journey. Turning to Aleryck, Taran jerks his chin at the honey-smeared tablet. "So, how does it work, then, little brother?"

Aleryck stares at him hard, before sighing and beckoning him over to the table. Taran sits down beside him. Aleryck slides the honey-smeared tablet over to him but doesn't let go. Taran's eyes widen. Silvery writing shines under the honey. He reads:

> *Deep within the mountain rift*
> *Find the hermit to claim your gift*
> *He will guide you in your task*
> *You won't receive if you don't ask.*

"What does it mean?" Taran asks. "Are we going to get a gift?"

Aleryck shoots him a look. "The message isn't for us, Taran," he says, snatching the tablet back. Standing abruptly, he limps over to the sink and starts scrubbing off the honey.

Taran drums his fingers on the table. He must admit the tablet is pretty cool. Possibly quite valuable? Hmm, there's a thought. He pushes himself away from the table. "Baydar! Noor! Seb! Kepler!" he yells. "Get yourselves ready. We're going on a journey."

Chapter 6--------SULPHUROUS STEAM

Aleryck jerks his head up as the pungent aroma hits his nostrils. Finally, they're here. It's been a long, tiring week, travelling all day by horseback, then camping out at night on the side of the road.

The first day, they'd only been on the road for an hour when they'd met Pa, on his way home. It'd been good seeing him again after so long and, of course, they had had to stop and explain to him what they were up to.

Aleryck straightens his back, re-living the scene when he'd told Pa about his special task from the Ancient: the pride in his pa's eyes almost makes all his aches and pains fade. Oh, and you should've seen the look on Taran's face! You could've brushed a cat with it, it was that prickly! Oho, he would put up with a sore butt any day to see that face again. Aleryck smiles at the memory.

Pa had given them his blessing to continue their journey, which was just as well, as Aleryck didn't know how he'd pull this thing off, otherwise. He'd rather not be spending so much time with Taran, but he does need his help right now, so he is just going to have to put up with him.

In the end, after the delay with Pa, they didn't get very far that first day. They'd reached Konia on the second day, but again were delayed, as both Ma and Pa had made them promise to stop by and see their elder brothers, Nash and Nerak. Not that he'd minded telling them about his quest. They, too, had admired his handwriting—he'd done a demonstration with a flame, which had gone down very well. Whilst it had felt weird being the centre of attention, he reckons he could get used to it.

But since then, the past five days have been completely uneventful. It's amazing how quickly the novelty of travelling wears off when you don't have a choice about it. It's getting to the point where he'd almost welcome seeing a snake. Even a Drifter, for that matter.

So, it's with great anticipation that Aleryck sniffs the air. At last, they've reached the Wastelands. He quickly covers his nose with his sleeve. It smells like rotten eggs. Pa told them it's the sulphur fumes leaking out of the ground.

"Phewee! Did you fart, Taran?" Baydar asks, sniggering.

"You sure do pong, Taran," Noor adds, dramatically flapping his hand in front of his nose. He's a bit too vigorous, and almost slips off his saddle.

The twins burst out laughing, and Aleryck grins.

Taran scowls at them all, before growling, "Shut up, you lot."

Boy, he sure has lost his sense of fun. What's eating him? Actually, Aleryck suspects he knows what's eating Taran. Taran's used to calling the shots, and now he's not. Oh well, it's not Aleryck's fault that the Ancient chose him and not Taran—that, for once, Aleryck is more important than Taran.

The road they're travelling skirts the foot of a hill that's been gradually growing to their right. The landscape to their left has transformed from orchards and vineyards at the outskirts of Konia, to farmland, then woodland. But now, as they round a corner, it changes again. The scraggly bushes finally give way to a carpet of reddish-brown dirt dotted with tussock grasses, bracken and brambles, and strewn with boulders.

Aleryck stops in his tracks and stares. There! A wisp of steam drifts out of the earth. Over there! More clouds waft heavenward. "Hey," he calls over his shoulder. "We've found it. Look—steam!"

Aleryck urges his donkey off the road towards the nearest tendril. The animal picks its way between the tussock grasses and the boulders. The sulphur smell grows stronger as they get closer. "Hurry up, Milly," Aleryck says, digging his heels into the donkey's flanks. The animal brays, breaks into a trot, then stops without warning. Aleryck, leaning forward in excitement, flies over Milly's neck and lands with a thump on the ground. He groans.

"Aleryck. Are you alright?" Baydar asks, hurrying over. He comes into view above Aleryck, who is sprawled on his back. Baydar's arm stretches towards him. "Let me help you up."

Aleryck grips the proffered hand and allows himself to be pulled to his feet.

"Watch out!" Baydar says, yanking Aleryck towards him.

"What?" Aleryck asks, alarmed.

Baydar inclines his chin towards something behind Aleryck. "There's a bit of a crack in the ground," he says.

Aleryck looks over his shoulder, then sags against his brother. *A bit of a crack?* That's an understatement. It's a massive fissure. If he'd fallen there, it would be quest over. No more Aleryck. "Uh, thanks Baydar."

By now the others have arrived. "What happened?" asks Kepler.

"Milly either just saved his life, or almost ended it," Baydar declares, waving an arm at the gaping drop.

"By the Ancient!" Kepler gasps, dropping to his stomach to peer over the edge. "Is this the Chasm?"

Seb sprawls beside his twin. "Cool!"

Taran snorts as he joins the group. "Don't be ridiculous. You need to brush up on your geography, little brothers. Medar—the Hole—is ages away from here. Like at least two days' travel in that direction." He gestures southwards.

Seb and Kepler scramble to their feet, brushing red dust off their clothes. "Yeah, Kepler," says Seb. "Can't believe you thought that was the Chasm."

Kepler plants his hands on his hips as he turns to his twin. "Well, you thought it was too!" he says.

"Did not."

"Did too." Kepler shoves Seb.

Seb shoves Kepler.

Next thing, they're locked together, rolling around on the ground, trying to throw punches. The fine red dust puffs around the flailing boys.

"Stop it," Aleryck says, hobbling towards them.

The twins tumble into Aleryck and he collapses on top of them with a cry.

"Alright, that's enough," Taran roars, grabbing one of the twin's thrashing arms. Baydar pulls Aleryck out of the fray.

Noor dives on top of the other twin, his lanky frame splayed like a net, pinning Seb to the ground. Or is it Kepler?

"Get off me."

"Promise you'll stop fighting?" Noor asks.

"Promise."

Noor rolls off the twin, who scrambles to his feet.

Meanwhile, Taran has pulled the other upright. If you couldn't tell them apart before, now it's impossible: twin dirt boys.

Noor's gaze flicks between them, then he bursts out laughing. Baydar guffaws and Aleryck starts giggling, too. Even Taran smiles. Noor clutches his tummy and doubles over; he's laughing so hard. "You should see yourselves!" he finally manages, flapping a hand in the dirt boys' direction.

"Alright Noor, that's enough," Taran says, clapping a hand on Noor's back. "Seb and Kepler, how about you both see if you can find some water—check that it's not too hot, first—and get yourselves cleaned up. The rest of us will find some steam to get this tablet thing done."

Aleryck scans his surroundings. "The steam I was aiming for, before I fell off the donkey, is on the other side of that fissure."

Baydar is leaning over, looking into the fissure. "There's steam coming out of the bottom of this crack. Look." He points.

They all peer over the lip. "I suppose that's as good as anything," Aleryck says. "But how will I get down? I can't climb."

"I could do it for you," Taran offers.

"No," Aleryck exclaims. "It's *my* tablet. The Ancient asked *me* to do it."

Taran's eyes narrow. "Fine," he snaps. He turns on his heel and strides to his horse. "I'll just be your slave and get everything for you then, shall I?"

"That would be good," says Aleryck. Taran needn't be so touchy. He'd promised Ma he'd help Aleryck, after all.

Shortly he returns with a coiled rope slung over his shoulder. "Right, let's get this rope around your waist, Aleryck. Lift your satchel up ... now under your arm ... oh. It's no good. Your satchel's in the way. You're going to have to take it off."

"What about my tablet?"

"We'll lower you down first," Taran says, "then you untie yourself, we'll pull the rope up, and lower down the tablet after."

Aleryck nods.

Once Aleryck is securely tied, Taran organises Baydar and Noor into a short chain-gang, with himself at the rear, his foot braced against a boulder. "Alright Aleryck, off you go," Taran says.

"Are you sure it's safe?" Aleryck asks.

"Only one way to find out," Taran says, grinning.

Aleryck scrambles back from the edge.

"I'm joking!" Taran calls.

Aleryck scowls, then creeps back to the fissure. He sits on the lip, then flips onto his stomach, legs dangling, bracing himself with his arms.

"Just let yourself slowly slide over the edge, Aleryck," Baydar says.

Aleryck takes a breath, then pushes himself over the edge. He hangs there. He lets out his breath. He's not falling. "Lower me," he says.

Gradually, he descends into the gap. He holds the rope at head level and pushes off the cliff face with his feet. He's just getting into a rhythm after ten bounds or so, when his feet touch the bottom. "I made it!" he calls.

"Untie yourself," Baydar says, his head appearing high above Aleryck.

Aleryck does as he's told.

The rope slithers upwards like a snake and disappears. A minute later, the tablet is lowered in his satchel. Aleryck reaches up and grabs it, so it won't get damaged as it lands. "Got it," he announces. He fumbles with the knot, but soon enough has extracted the tablet. He flips back the goatskin—*yep, the stylus is still there. Good.* He set off towards the steam that drifts from around a corner in the narrow cleft, not far ahead.

As he rounds the corner, the pungent fumes catch in the back of his throat, and he coughs, his eyes watering. A cloud of steam wafts over him, and he staggers against the rocky wall, spluttering and heaving.

"Are you alright?" one of his brothers asks, his voice echoing from far above.

Aleryck can't see who it is, but it sounds like Noor. "Yes," he croaks, "I think so." Hopes so. *Better get on with it, though.* He unwraps the tablet, picks up the stylus, and sits on a small boulder poking out of the ground. He closes his eyes. *Ancient?* he calls with his mind.

"I'm here, Aleryck," the Ancient says. "Here are the next words." The Ancient says them in his mind, a stanza at a time, waiting for Aleryck to write the words, before giving him the next line:

> *Go up Helix River, to its source*
> *At the waterfall—a powerful force—*

Follow the sounds of birds up high
Of honey bees buzzing as they fly
When sunlight fades to shades of grey
At dusk watch for nature's display
From whence the cloud comes, will reveal
The path which is elsewise concealed

He writes as fast as he can, but even so, he must regularly dash out of the steam to gulp a lungful of fresh air before plunging back into the fumes. It doesn't help that his brothers keep on calling down from above, "Are you done yet?" or "When will you be finished?". They must've got bored asking though, because after a while it goes quiet.

Finally, he writes the word 'concealed' and the task is complete. He staggers out of the cloud, and leans against the wall, sucking in deep breaths. He limps back to where the rope is dangling and, after wrapping the goatskin around the tablet and stylus, ties the bundled tablet to the end. He tugs the rope a couple of times. "You can pull it up now," he calls.

Silence.

"Guys! Taran? Baydar?"

A giggle.

"Hey, it's not funny. Pull up the tablet. Now!" he demands.

The rope slithers up like a snake, and Seb's face appears above him, grinning. He obviously found some water to wash off all that dust. "It *is* funny," he insists.

The tablet disappears over the lip, and so does Seb's face. He hears some scuffling and giggling. He waits. And waits. "Taran, where's the rope?"

No response.

"Taran. Now it's really not funny. Drop down the rope! C'mon, Baydar. Noor? Someone?" Aleryck closes his eyes and strains his ears. He can't hear anything. What are they up to? He puts his hands on his hips and cranes his neck, staring at the ribbon of sky overhead. The light is fading, and a lone star twinkles high above.

He steps back and leans against the wall, then slides down until he's sitting on the ground. Fine, Taran's playing another one of his pranks on him. Well, he's used to it. He can wait. Taran'll come back for him. *Won't he?*

He waits and waits. As the sky darkens overhead, a tear leaks out of the corner of his eye. Suddenly, he is angry. He brushes away the tear with his sleeve. Why has the Ancient abandoned him? He promised that he'd be with Aleryck every step of the way. Throwing his head back, he screams, "WHY HAVE YOU LEFT ME?"

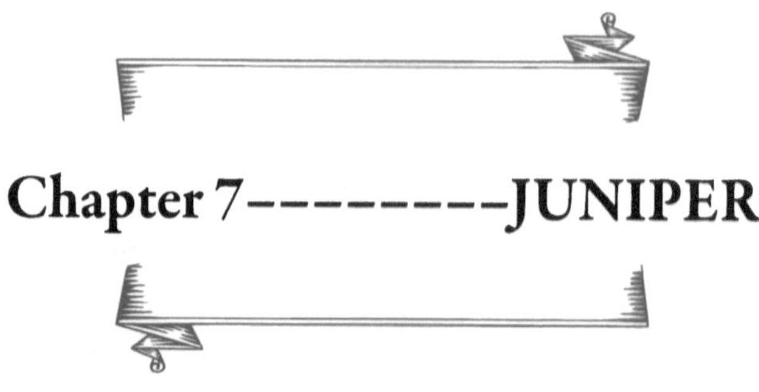

Chapter 7———————JUNIPER

Juniper laughs as she leaps from rock to rock, sure-footed as a goat. Her long black hair flows behind her, the curls bouncing off her shoulders as though they're jumping too.

Her people lead a wandering existence amongst these rocky places, and navigating the uneven surface is as natural as breathing for Juniper. At sixteen, she's the eldest daughter of the clan's priestess, and should probably be doing something more useful, like collecting water or helping in the temple. But this morning when she woke, she heard the Ancient calling her to this place. And when the Ancient calls, she follows. This isn't the first time, and she's told her mother, so she knows her family won't worry.

It's late afternoon when she senses she's arrived. She catches movement out of the corner of her eye and drops to a crouch. Far below, a road hugs the base of the mountain. Beyond the road stretch the Wastelands. Usually, they are deserted. Why would anyone have a need to go there? But that is where the movement came from—not too far off the road. And it's not just the drifts of steam. She squints to improve her vision. Yep. It's definitely people. Maybe five? And as many horses. Strange. They're heading towards the road and appear to be in good spirits. But where have they come from?

She feels compelled to go to them. With a whistle to her hawk, Aya, circling high above, Juniper begins her descent. In her sand-coloured tunic and breeches, she knows she is well-camouflaged from human eyes, but Aya will have no problem seeing her.

She's almost at the road when another sound reaches her ears. Baritone voices and the rumble of multiple horses' hooves, coming from over a rise behind her, where a rocky outcrop forces the road into a sharp bend. She skips behind a boulder and peers over. Oh no. Slavers! And a large group of them, at that. That small band of people coming out of the Wastelands is heading straight for them. She shuts her eyes and takes a few deep breaths. Is this what the Ancient called her here for?

"No. It is something else," whispers the Ancient's voice in her mind.

Surprised, her eyes pop open. Alright then, she'll watch and wait.

The small group reach the road below her. She counts them: five boys plus five horses. Juniper can hear them clearly.

"Hey, Taran," one of the younger ones says. He has the squeaky voice of a boy changing into manhood. "That was a great prank. Shall we go back and get him now?"

The one called Taran appears to be the leader. He's taller than the rest and has the nicest horse. He's not bad looking, either. "Oh, I dunno," he says. "Maybe we should leave him just a little bit longer. Might give him time to realise he's not as special as he thinks." He spits the word 'special'.

Juniper raises an eyebrow.

"C'mon, bro," says another. That one sounds older than the first. "It's long enough. I'm going back for him." He turns to head back into the Wastelands.

At that very moment, the Slavers round the corner.

Juniper shrinks back behind her boulder.

"Oho, what do we have here?" says a Slaver. There is a jingle of harnesses as he dismounts.

"Hey, what are you doing?" says the one called Taran. "Don't touch my horse."

"Your horse? I think it's mine, now," says the same Slaver.

There is a rumble of laughter. Not nice laughter.

Juniper risks a peek around the boulder. The Slavers have all dismounted and surround the small group of boys. By the looks of the small group, she guesses they're brothers. Several of the Slavers have grabbed the bridles of their horses and pulled the brothers to the ground. They look scared.

Except for Taran. He faces the Slaver, his hands held open, palms up. "Hey," he says, "we're just some poor farmers. We're not worth that much."

The head Slaver smiles, one of his teeth glinting silver. His hair is tied back into a ponytail and is jet black, matching his black breeches and riding cloak. The only splash of colour is a wide, scarlet sash tied at his waist, through which is thrust a long, curved sabre. "I think we'll leave it up to the market to decide how much you're worth," he drawls. "Besides, you all look very strong."

"What about Aleryck?" asks one of the younger brothers.

The Slaver raises an eyebrow. "Who is Aleryck?"

Taran shoots a glare at the brother who spoke. "We're supposed to be meeting him in Konia," he says in a loud voice. "He'll wonder where we are if we don't show up tonight."

The Slaver smirks. "Yes, I imagine he will. Too bad. Round 'em up!" The Slaver circles his finger in the air.

"Wait," Taran says. "I have something more valuable than us. We can trade."

The Slaver pauses. "Yes?"

"It's in my saddle bag." At a nod from the Slaver, Taran turns to his horse and digs around in the saddle bag. He pulls out something the size of a book, wrapped in goatskin.

The Slaver snatches it out of his hands.

"Careful!" Taran says.

The Slaver flips open the goatskin.

Juniper cranes her neck but can't see what's inside. She needn't have bothered. The Slaver holds the object aloft, exclaiming, "Gentlemen, behold, a block of glass!" He hoots with laughter and the other Slavers all join in, slapping their thighs and whooping.

"It's not what you think," Taran shouts over the ruckus. "It's a magical tablet."

A tingle runs down Juniper's spine at those words.

The head Slaver makes a slashing motion with his hand, and everyone stops laughing. He steps up to Taran, such that they're almost nose to nose. "Good try," he sneers. He spins on his heel, flicking a hand above his head. "Round them up," he says again, handing the tablet to one of his men. "Put that somewhere safe."

"No," Taran shouts, straining against the hold of the two Slavers who have grabbed him. "Don't take us. Or, only take me and set my brothers free!" He cranes his neck to stare back at the Wastelands.

What's he looking for? Juniper wonders.

But Taran's attempts to bargain freedom for his brothers are to no avail. Juniper watches as Taran and the brothers' hands are tied and all of them are lashed together. Some of the Slavers leap onto the brothers' horses, but many are still on foot.

They set off in the opposite direction to Konia, their new captives in tow.

Chapter 8--------A CRY FOR HELP

Juniper waits until the dust has settled before climbing down from her hiding place and crossing the road. The sun has dropped below the mountain, and a single star hangs in the heavens. "What now?" she asks out loud.

Her bird Aya screeches far above and flies out over the Wastelands.

"Go into the Wastelands," the Ancient speaks into her mind.

That's a strong signal. She heads into the red, rocky landscape at a trot, conscious that this place will be treacherous in the dark.

She stops to listen. What was that? A sort of sniffling sound. Then, from out of the ground ahead of her, issues a wail—

"WHY HAVE YOU LEFT ME?"

She hurries forward. A dark gash scars the ground ahead. She slows her pace.

"You asked me to do this task, and I did it! Why have you let this happen to me?" the voice demands.

She drops to her belly and slithers forwards to peer into the crack. "Who are you talking to?" she asks.

The voice yelps. Then asks, "Who are you?"

"I'm Juniper. What in the name of the Ancient are you doing down there?"

"My rotten brothers left me down here and I don't think they're coming back."

"I can tell you for certain that they aren't coming back."

"Huh? How do you know that?"

"Well, if the group of five boys with horses were your brothers, then they just got captured by Slavers. They're headed off towards Beta."

"What? Oh no. I have to get to them. Can you help me out?"

"Sure. How?"

"Did they leave the rope up there? Please tell me they did."

Juniper spies the rope lying on the ground not too far away. "They did," she says.

"Thank the Ancient," says the boy, relief in his voice.

"There's something else here, too. A bag by the looks."

"Is there anything in it?" The boy's voice sounds desperate.

Juniper checks the bag. "Just a flint and a mouldy piece of cheese," she informs him.

"That thieving toad!"

"I beg your pardon?"

"Nothing. Just get me out of here, will you?"

Juniper feeds the rope down into the crevice. After a short while she feels a tug.

"You can pull me up now ... can you? Are you strong enough?" There's a note of panic in the voice.

Juniper snorts. "Why, are you very heavy?"

"No!"

"Well then, there's no problem. Shall we do this?" Wrapping the rope around her waist then over her shoulder, she braces herself and heaves on the rope. Slowly, slowly, she inches away from the fissure. She doesn't dare let go a hand to feed the rope backwards. She might be strong, but even she can't take the boy's weight with one hand.

Her heel hits a rock, and she stumbles, landing heavily on her butt. The rope whips through her palms, burning them. She screams and lets go.

"Aargh!" The boy's scream echoes her own and is followed by a thud.

Juniper scrambles back to the fissure, slamming her knee down on the rope to prevent it going any further. "I'm sorry," she gasps. "Are you alright?"

"Yes," says the boy. "What happened?"

"I tripped. And now ..." She inspects her palms.

"Now what?" comes the anxious reply.

"... now I've burned my palms and I don't think I can pull you up." She peers over the lip. "I'm so sorry," she repeats.

At that moment, a donkey brays nearby.

Juniper jumps, her hand to her heart. "By the Ancient! That gave me a fright."

"My donkey," the boy exclaims. "Can you get her to help?"

Juniper sucks in her breath. "Good idea. I'll be back." She secures the end of the rope to a large rock then checks where the braying came from. The donkey is several kama away. She approaches the animal slowly, crooning, "Hello girl. Come and help me."

The donkey takes a step towards her, then noses the ground to nibble at a clump of wiry tussock.

Juniper takes another cautious step towards it. Then another.

The donkey's ears flick, but the animal continues its attack on the plant.

Reaching the donkey, Juniper shoots out a hand and grabs the reins dangling from the harness. "Yes!" she crows in triumph.

The donkey jerks her head up and, braying loudly, turns and drags Juniper several steps.

Juniper holds on tight, gritting her teeth against the pain in her hands, and digs her heels into the ground. "Whoa, girl," she soothes. *Keep calm, Juniper!*

The donkey stops, watching her.

"It's alright. We're just going to go for a little walk."

"Hey, what's the hold up?" the boy's voice echoes from the crevice.

The donkey flicks her ears towards her master's voice, and trots forwards at pace.

"Attagirl," Juniper says. Then, pitching her voice in the boy's direction, adds, "Just bringing your donkey now." She pulls a face. No need to tell him the donkey's actually bringing her.

The boy calls out, "Come on Milly. I'm down here."

Milly steps to the edge of the crevice, ears twitching.

Perfect. Without releasing the reins, Juniper swiftly picks up the rope. She ties it to the donkey's harness and tests the knot. It's tight. "Good girl, Milly," she says. She checks on Aleryck. "Are you still tied on?"

"Yep."

To the donkey she says, "Now, let's pull your master up." She walks away from the crevice, tugging on the rope to turn Milly's head.

Milly resists, standing stubbornly on the spot.

Juniper tries again. "Come on. This way."

The donkey looks at her but doesn't move.

Juniper plants her hands on her hips and narrows her eyes at Milly. *Now what?*

Aya chooses that moment to swoop down from the twilight skies and lands on Juniper's shoulder with a screech.

Startled, Milly brays and bolts away from the crevice, dragging Juniper with her. Aya flaps off in alarm.

"Aargh!" the boy yells, as he's dragged upwards.

Juniper stumbles and lands heavily on her stomach, but doesn't let go of the reins. She couldn't even if she wanted to; they're tangled around her wrist.

As suddenly as she started, Milly stops.

Juniper lies on the ground for a minute, groaning. Everything hurts. She wriggles her toes. Bruised, but not broken then. She rolls to her knees. Spitting dirt out of her mouth, she stands and eyes Milly.

Milly stares back, all innocence, as if to say, "What did I do?"

Juniper scowls at Milly as she works the reins loose from her wrist.

"Hello? Some help here please?" comes a muffled voice from behind her.

Oh, yes. The boy! "I'm coming." Flinging the rein aside, Juniper dashes to the crevice. The boy is clinging to the rope, half out of the crevice, face down. He lifts his head. His face is covered in blood. She grabs his arms and hauls him all the way out.

"Are you alright?" she asks.

He lies on the ground for a second before rolling onto his back. "Thank you, Juniper," he finally manages, as he pushes himself to a sitting position.

"You're welcome ... what's your name?"

"Aleryck," he says.

Calm floods her mind. *You are here for him.*

"Oh. *You're* Aleryck." She squints at him. The light is fading rapidly, and she can't really make out his features. "I thought you were in Konia?"

"What? And how do you know my name?"

Juniper tucks a strand of hair behind her ear. "It's a long story. It's getting dark. We need to get out of these Wastelands. Let's do proper introductions somewhere safer, shall we? C'mon, Aleryck." She extends him a hand and pulls him to his feet.

He immediately collapses to the ground with a cry, rubbing one of his legs.

"Oh, you're injured! Why didn't you tell me?" She drops to her knees beside him, reaching to check his leg.

"I'm okay," he mutters, fending off her arm. "Or rather, I'm not injured. I've got a bad leg, is all."

"Oh," she says. She looks him over. He doesn't seem very strong. "Shall I help you get on to Milly?"

"No," he says sharply. He tries to stand but stumbles once more. "I mean, yes." He hangs his head.

She pulls his arm around her shoulder and heaves him upright. As they shuffle towards Milly, Juniper frowns. "Why in the name of Tyrelia did your brothers put you down that crevice? Is it because you were slowing them down?"

There's a sharp intake of breath. "No," Aleryck says. "I asked to get put down there."

Juniper stops dead in her tracks. "What?" she asks. "Why?"

"It was for the tablet. I needed to get to some sulphurous steam."

Juniper shakes her head. "You're not making any sense. What tablet?"

Aleryck sighs. "It's complicated."

"Well then, it's lucky I've got plenty of time. Look, here's Milly. Let's get that rope off you." She works the knot at his waist until it comes free, then helps Aleryck onto the donkey.

"My satchel!" he exclaims. "Can you get it, please?"

She scans the ground and spots it not too far away. She picks it up and hands it to Aleryck, who slips it over his head.

"Now, let's get out of here. We need to find some shelter, make a fire, and eat," says Juniper. She lifts her chin and lets out a piercing whistle. From the twilight, Aya plunges towards them, a dark form dangling from her talons. "Well done, Aya, you caught us a rabbit," Juniper coos gently to the bird, bending down to retrieve the prey the hawk has dropped at her feet. Aya settles on Juniper's shoulder, and they set off.

∞∞∞∞∞

Half an hour later, they're seated around a small fire in the shelter of several boulders, with the rabbit cooking on a stick above the flames. It smells really good.

"So, Aleryck," Juniper says, leaning back against a rock. "Tell me about this tablet."

Aleryck rubs his leg absent-mindedly as he recounts his calling by the Ancient and all the different clues he's inscribed on the tablet. "The last clue had to be inscribed in sulphurous steam. Of course, for that I needed to go to the Wastelands, and there was no way I could make the journey by myself," Aleryck says, waving a hand at his bad leg.

Juniper nods, understanding in her eyes. "But that doesn't explain why they left you down that fissure," she says, leaning forward.

Aleryck drops his head. "That may be partly my fault," he mumbles.

"How?"

"Well, I may have been a little … rude. To Taran."

"How do you mean?"

Aleryck fiddles with the strap of his satchel. "I might've been a bit demanding. Ordering him around." He jerks his head up. "He's always been the bossy one. He's strong and confident. Since Nerak and Nash left home, he's the eldest, and all of my brothers do whatever he says—even if it's not right. He can be very charming when he wants. So, when the Ancient called me—me!—to inscribe the tablet, it made me feel special. Important. For once, I was the centre of attention. And I liked it!" He looks Juniper straight in the eye, challenging her to deny him these feelings.

Juniper just nods, sitting cross-legged, her hands resting in her lap. The firelight flickers across her features. "Remember I told you that I saw the Slavers capture your brothers?" she asks.

"Yes."

"I also saw Taran trying to bargain their way out of being captured by trading their release with your tablet."

"What?" Aleryck gasps. "What happened?"

Juniper frowns. "They seemed to think it was just a block of glass, and not that valuable. They put it in one of the horse's saddlebags."

Aleryck's shoulders slump. "Now I'll never get the tablet back! I've failed the Ancient. What am I going to do?" he wails.

Juniper reaches over and touches his shoulder. "Aleryck," she says, "I wasn't sure when I first met you, but now I know why the Ancient told me to go to you."

Aleryck's head whips up. "What?" he breathes. "The Ancient spoke to you too?"

Juniper nods. "Yep. He sent me here to help you. Because this is not a one-person task."

Aleryck breaks into a smile. "The Ancient said he would help me. That I wouldn't have to do this alone. I never thought that he meant he'd send someone like you."

Juniper gently shoves his shoulder. "What do you mean 'someone like me'? You mean a Drifter?"

"No!" Aleryck protests. "I mean someone as pretty and clever as you." *Curds!* He hadn't meant it to come out like that. Heat floods his cheeks.

Juniper's eyes soften. She leans back against the rock, a smile curving her lips. "Why, thank you Aleryck. That's a big compliment from someone as ... rude as you." She chuckles.

Aleryck doesn't know what to say. He's never met a girl like this before. Come to think of it, he's hardly met any girls at all. Either way, he can't imagine any girl being smarter, funnier, or more beautiful than Juniper. *And* she knows the Ancient's voice. He shakes his head in wonder.

Juniper's voice breaks into his thoughts. "So, tomorrow we'll need to track down those Slavers and get your brothers and the tablet back. Let's get some sleep. I suspect it will be a tiring day."

Chapter 9---------THE SLAVERS

When they finally come to a halt, Taran drops to his knees. They've been walking for six days now, all the time getting further and further from Konia. Further from any chance of anyone finding them. Would anyone even be looking? Probably not. Nerak and Nash wouldn't be expecting to see them again for at least another three weeks as they know that, after completing the sulphurous steam writing, he and the rest of them were heading into The Hole to hide the tablet somewhere—which they'd expected to take a couple of weeks. Then they would need to reverse the journey. It was hopeless to think they would suspect that anything was wrong. No help was coming anytime soon.

And what about Aleryck? The poor kid has as much chance of getting out of that crevice by himself as a goat does of flying. If Taran ever manages to escape, he'll go straight back to that crevice and get Aleryck out. Hopefully he'll still be alive. And then? Aleryck would ask about the tablet. That thing was what got them into this mess to start with. But he would definitely need to get it; no point in rescuing Aleryck without it. And what if Aleryck is ... dead? Taran hangs his head. He could never go back home again. What would he tell Ma? Taran blinks unbidden tears away. Horses' teeth, he's made a mess of things. Well, he'll do whatever he needs to, to make things right.

"Get up," a Slaver snarls, hauling Taran to his feet by the rope binding his hands.

Taran grits his teeth and stumbles behind the Slaver to a big tree where his brothers are also being herded. They're forced to sit with their backs to the trunk whilst their feet are bound. Then a rope is tied around each waist and secured to another rope encircling the base of the tree. This has been the drill each night. There's no escaping—the Ancient knows they've tried. He wishes they would untie his hands, though. His wrists ache from the coarse rope chafing against them all day and cutting into his skin.

The leader of the Slavers swaggers towards them, rubbing his hands together with a wide smile on his face. The other Slavers call him Slasher. Taran suspects he knows why but would rather not find out first-hand. "Well, boys," Slasher says, "tomorrow's the big day. We're on the outskirts of Beta here, and tomorrow we'll see what you all fetch at the slave auction."

Next to him, Seb whimpers. Or is it Kepler?

Slasher turns on his heel, calling to his men. "Alright, you lot, empty out all the saddle bags and let's see what we've got. Might be able to shift some items at the market while we're here."

Whilst two men spread out some woven mats on the ground, four others work their way through all the horses, including the brothers' ones, collecting the saddle bags, and dumping the contents onto the mats. Over the past week, Taran has learned that the Slavers had acquired horses and other loot from Konia before they'd captured him and his brothers.

The pile grows higher and higher. There! Taran leans forward as the tablet tumbles out of one of the satchels and slides down the pile like a miniature toboggan. It comes to rest on one of its sides, nestled between a bolt of bright blue fabric and a bronze candlestick.

Baydar, seated to Taran's left, elbows him in the ribs. "The tablet," he whispers.

"Yeah, I see it," Taran murmurs in reply. He can't get it, though. Even if he wriggles down as far as the rope around his waist will allow, he'll still be a body's-length away from the corner of the mat.

Meanwhile, other Slavers are setting up Slasher's tent—a big square affair with tassels around the edges, propped up on poles. Carpets and cushions cover the ground on the inside. Obviously, being the leader of this band of villains is a lucrative business.

The men finish tipping out the plunder, and seat themselves cross-legged in a rough semi-circle at one end of the pile, not too far from where Taran and his brothers lie trussed.

One of the Slavers eyes the sky where the sun hangs low above the horizon. "It'll start getting dark in an hour," he states. "Let's get cracking. Hey, Scarface!" he yells over his shoulder.

A burly man who's been watering the horses turns at the call. "Sir?" he asks.

"When you're done there, can you get a fire going?"

"Sure thing, Bones" Scarface says. Before long, he builds the fire in the middle of the camp site, about half-way between Slasher's tent and where Bones is sitting.

Bones and the others start digging through the pile of loot. They work in pairs, with two grabbing an item each out of the pile, then passing it to their partner, who inspects it closely before putting it in one of two new piles. Taran guesses the piles were for the valuable and the valueless. *Which pile will the tablet end up in?* he wonders.

Scarface and a Slaver called Cookie start preparing dinner. They peel some root vegetables, dug out of someone's garden, and chuck them in a pot of water on the fire, before adding chunks of meat from some animal. Taran would bet his boot they rustled the animal from some unlucky farmer. Before long a delicious aroma fills the air. Taran's stomach grumbles loudly. Around him, his brothers start shuffling upright in anticipation of being fed.

Taran keeps his eye on the tablet. The mountain of spoils has dwindled to the last few objects, one of which is the tablet. But it's also getting darker now that the sun has dropped behind the mountain in the distance.

Bones reaches for the tablet and glances at it briefly, before handing it to his partner, Twotoes. "Worthless," he says.

Taran lets out a breath.

Twotoes places it on the 'worthless' pile but, as he does so, the face catches the firelight and, instantly, silvery writing shimmers on the surface. He gasps. "Bones, look!" he exclaims, thrusting the tablet back at Bones.

Bones grabs the tablet. "What's this?" he says. He stares at the words, then slowly reads them aloud:

"Tyrelia! Land of gold
A land so lovely to behold
O, land of beauty, land of light
Joyous refuge, pure delight
Tyrelia! That land so fair
Of meadows green and clean pure air
Of stately trees in forests vast
Of ancient rocks from ages past

"Well, well, well. That's a pretty poem." He rubs his sleeve over the tablet, but the words shine as brightly as ever. "Daggers!" he says. "We could fetch some coin for this! I'd better show Slasher." Bones jumps up, strides over to Slasher's tent and disappears inside.

"Well, that just complicated things," Taran mutters to Baydar.

A lantern from within casts Bones' and Slasher's shadows onto the tent wall. It reminds Taran of one of those shadow-puppet plays they saw as kids at the annual fair in Konia. The voices talk indistinctly, followed by an exclamation of surprise. One of the shadow-puppets opens a chest and lays the tablet in it, before locking it with a key.

Slasher emerges from his tent, a grin on his face, rubbing his hands together. "New plan," he announces loud enough for all to hear. "Tomorrow, we head to the treasure markets in Gamma."

Murmurs rise from the Slavers, but no one challenges Slasher.

Gamma? Taran pictures a map of Tyrelia in his mind's eye. Gamma is off to the west of the Hole. Gotta be at least another week's march to get there. His heart sinks at the prospect. Then almost immediately buoys again. That gives them more time to escape! And, more importantly, more time to get their hands on the tablet so he can make amends with Aleryck.

A flicker of hope kindles in his heart.

Chapter 10--------PILLARS AND GATES

Aleryck hobbles to catch up to Juniper. "Are you sure this is going to work?" he asks.

Juniper turns her head, causing her long braid to flick over her shoulder. "Yes, of course it will work. I've done it hundreds of times."

"Hundreds?"

"Well, maybe not *hundreds*. But plenty. It's not so bad once you get used to it."

"And you're sure it's alright for me to do it, even though I'm not part of your priestly clan?" Aleryck cuts his eyes at Juniper.

She stops and places her hands on Aleryck's shoulders, gazing into his eyes. "Aleryck, the Ancient's gifts have been given to *all* the inhabitants of Tyrelia to enjoy. Just because most people don't know about warping, doesn't mean they're not allowed to do it. This is something my people discovered and, I'll admit, we have kept it a secret. But now,"—she moves one hand to poke Aleryck's chest—"you and I are on the Ancient's business. The Ancient sent me to help you, and I'm convinced this is why: You can't walk long distances. I have the key to travelling long distances in the blink of an eye. It makes perfect sense." She turns on her heel and keeps walking.

Aleryck nods slowly. "I suppose you're right. Are you sure we can't take Milly, though?" He glances behind him. They've left Milly grazing in a copse of trees. He can't see her, and hopes she'll be alright.

"We've been over this Aleryck. No, we can't."

"But you're taking Aya." He pouts.

Juniper makes a noise of exasperation. "She a bird. She sits on my shoulder. We can't carry a donkey."

Aleryck sighs. "I know." He hitches his satchel up to rest more comfortably on his shoulder, then shades his eyes, peering into the distance ahead. "Is that the Law Pillar?"

"Yep, that's it. Come on. Not far now."

As they hurry towards it, the pillar grows in girth and stature, until it is towering above them, its shadow a pathway for them to follow.

Aleryck cranes his neck, trying to make out the writing on its surface. He knows what the words will say: there are many Law Pillars in Tyrelia, and everyone learns the laws off by heart from a young age. Even so, it's still exciting to see them up close—it's been a long time since he's bothered to read one. He vaguely recalls seeing one in Konia as they passed through, but it had been several blocks away from where they stayed with his brothers.

The sand-coloured pillar is so broad at the base that it would take him and all his brothers linking hands to encircle it. The words are etched at about eye-level, four times around the structure. Aleryck reads them aloud:

THE LAWS OF TYRELIA

1. Honour the Ancient
2. Put others first
3. Use your gifts for good
4. Follow the Rules

Whistling to Aya, Juniper joins him and takes his hand. Aleryck shoots her a look, but she's got her eyes shut and is frowning. Aya lands on her shoulder and Juniper grips Aya's talons.

"What're you doing?" Aleryck asks.

"Shh," Juniper says. "I'm trying to concentrate. Stay still and don't let go of my hand."

Aleryck's good with that. Her hand is warm and strong. He likes holding it. He smiles.

His smile freezes as the world spins around him. He's sucked into a tunnel of air and, for a second, feels weightless. Then he's falling and he loses his balance. Only Juniper's grip prevents him from landing flat on his face. He screams.

"Aleryck! We're here. We're alright."

Aleryck snaps his mouth shut and breathes hard through his nose. He's on his hands and knees on grass, at the base of a Law Pillar next to a forest. He scrambles to his feet and turns slowly on the spot. "By the Ancient," he says. "We've travelled to another pillar!"

Juniper slaps him on the back. "It's called warping, and we sure have. This is the Beta Gate Law Pillar. And that,"—she spins to point in the opposite direction to the forest—"is the Beta Gate."

Aleryck gasps. An ancient archway, formed of roughly hewn rocks, stands abandoned in the middle of a meadow. There is no wall either side, no building that the archway leads to. Just the archway. "What's it doing there?" Aleryck asks.

"That, Aleryck, is another closely guarded secret."

Aleryck barks a laugh. "I hate to point this out to you, Juniper, but it's not a very well-hidden secret." He grins at his own wit.

Juniper punches him lightly on his shoulder. "Not the archway, smart breeches. It marks a secret pathway into Medar."

Aleryck turns to stare at the arch. "Really?"

"Yep." She positions herself between the Law Pillar and the arch, and spreads her arms wide, one pointing at the Law Pillar, the other at the arch. "Line yourself up like this and follow that direction to the Chasm. That's where the top of the staircase will be."

"That's so cool. I was wondering how we would get into the Hole."

"Well, now you know." Juniper turns back to the forest. "But our path leads this way. Whilst warping to this pillar has saved us a few days, we've still got about four days' walk through the forest to get to Beta. With any luck we'll get there before the Slavers."

"Couldn't we have warped directly to Beta? Surely there's a Law Pillar in Beta itself?"

"Technically we could. But then people might see us arrive, and that would cause a few problems that we don't want to deal with right now. We still need to keep this way of travelling secret. Besides, the Slavers won't get to Beta for at least another four days, so this way we should arrive just in time to intercept them."

Aleryck sighs as he trudges after her. She's right again.

∞∞∞∞∞

They've been travelling for three days since arriving at the Beta Gate Law Pillar and all Aleryck can think about is Taran and his stupid trick. If Taran hadn't interfered, then they could've already hidden the tablet in Medar and be safely on their way home by now. But no. Taran had to take the tablet, and now look where it got them. When they reach the Slavers, Aleryck will need to get that tablet back, but they can keep Taran for all he cares. A pang of remorse stabs though him. Yes, he feels bad for his other brothers. They probably don't deserve to be sold as slaves. But that would serve them right for blindly following Taran. Besides, he can't go rescuing them all AND get the tablet safely into Medar. Can he? He shakes his head. *Impossible.*

Aleryck is snapped out of his reverie by Juniper's exclamation. "By the Ancient!" She is staring at the ground, walking in a large circle.

"What is it?"

Juniper points. "See this? The grass is all trampled. Many people have camped here." She walks over to a patch of charred ground in the centre and pokes it with the toe of her boot. A dull red glows from amongst the black and grey remains. "This was their campfire. It's still warm, so they likely only left this morning." She strides over to some trees and drops to her knees. "There were horses here. At least ten from what I can tell."

Aleryck limps over to Juniper and stares at the ground. "You can tell that from a bit of flattened grass?" he asks. *Incredible.*

"Well, not just the grass. You can feel hoof marks if you run your fingers over the ground. The grass is all nibbled off in a row here. And look at that." Juniper points to the trees. "The bark is rubbed off there, there and there, so that's where the horses were tied to the trees."

"Oh."

Juniper jumps up and disappears behind a large tree off to the side. She whistles. "Check this out, Aleryck."

He hobbles around to see what she's found. He stops in his tracks. It's a pile of stuff: some clothing, a broken clay pot, a stick...

"Hey! That's my stylus!" Aleryck exclaims, crouching to grab it. "They've taken the gemstone. But maybe the tablet's here, too?" He feverishly scrabbles through the small pile, discarding items as soon he picks them up. "Here's the goatskin wrapping," he says. He extracts it and places it next to the stylus. His body sags. "It's not here."

Juniper places a hand on his shoulder. "Well, at least it's not all bad news," she says.

Aleryck frowns. "What do you mean it's not all bad news? This isn't good news." He waves the useless stylus and goatskin wrapping at Juniper.

"But it is," Juniper insists. "For one, we know for sure this was the Slaver camp. Secondly, we know they only left this morning. And thirdly, we know they didn't go to Beta."

This last statement surprises Aleryck. "We do?"

"We do," Juniper confirms, hauling Aleryck to his feet and grabbing his free hand. She drags him over to another swathe of trampled grass. "This is the direction they left in. They're headed to Gamma."

"How do you know?"

"There's nothing else in this direction. It's got to be Gamma. If we leave now, we might catch up to them."

Aleryck sighs. He just wants to rest. But Juniper is right. They can't stop now. He carefully wraps the goatskin around the stylus and tucks it into his satchel. "Alright. I'm ready," he says.

Chapter 11--------THE GAMMA GATE

Two days, they'd wasted. Two whole days. Just to end up back where they'd started five days earlier: at the Beta Gate Pillar. It had been promising initially. Juniper was a good tracker, and the trail was obvious. But Aleryck's leg had hampered them. He tired quickly and needed to rest and massage out the kinks. By yesterday evening, Juniper had declared they would turn back.

"It's obvious from their tracks that they're travelling parallel to the Chasm," she'd said, "which means they'll end up practically at the Gamma Gate Pillar in five days' time."

"Will they?" Aleryck asked.

"Yes, the pillar is on the road to Gamma. I'm sure that's the route they're planning to take. And we can beat them there. But it does mean that we're going to have to turn back."

So now, here they are.

"Are you ready?" Juniper asks, grabbing his hand.

Aleryck gulps. "Yeah, I think so," he says. He squeezes his eyes shut.

Even though he's prepared this time, it doesn't prevent him from heaving and gagging upon arrival at the Gamma Gate Pillar. He opens his eyes and wipes his clammy forehead with his sleeve. "I don't think I'll ever get used to that."

Juniper smiles at him as she helps him to his feet. "Sure you will, Aleryck. It took me about ten times before I stopped puking. And look at you—you haven't even puked once!"

"*Now* you tell me," he mutters. He looks at his surroundings. "Did we not leave the Beta Gate Pillar yet?"

Juniper plants her hands on her hips. "What do you mean? That," she points emphatically, "is the Gamma Gate Pillar."

"How can you be sure? It looks exactly the same as the Beta Gate one."

"Don't be silly." Juniper laughs. "It's quite different. For starters, you can tell from the position of the sun and its shadow, that it's to the west of the Chasm, not the north."

Aleryck studies the sun and the shadow relative to the scrubby bushes that mark the Chasm's edge. "Alright, we're at the Gamma Gate Pillar." He scratches his head. "Now what?"

"We need to make a plan for how to free your brothers and get your tablet back, once the Slavers turn up."

Aleryck straightens his back. "About that ..."

"Yes?"

He clears his throat. "Getting the tablet is the most important thing. I mean, if we have to choose between my brothers and the tablet ... well, we choose the tablet." The last part comes out in a rush.

Juniper raises an eyebrow and stares at him for a while, before responding. "If that's what you want. But there's no 'we'. Don't be mad, Aleryck, but I think it will be best if you stay here—well hidden—and I go and get the tablet by myself. I'll likely have to make a fast getaway and, well ..." Her eyes drop to his bad leg.

Aleryck reaches up and squeezes her hand. "I get it, Juniper. I'm not mad. Besides, someone needs to find the stairway."

"That's a good idea, Aleryck. I'm going to scout back towards Beta and see if I can spot any sign of the Slavers coming." She shades her eyes as she scans the skies for her bird and lets out a piercing whistle. Aya dives from the heavens to land on Juniper's outstretched arm. "We'll be back before nightfall."

Aleryck raises a hand in farewell and watches her retreating figure for many minutes, before turning towards the Gamma Gate. He hitches up his breeches, then sets off.

Unlike the Beta Gate, which stands in the middle of a meadow, this one is set amongst the scrubby bushes that line the edge of the Chasm. Aleryck reaches the first of the bushes. They're almost as tall as him. He presses into the foliage. The many, tiny green leaves fool him into thinking they are soft, so he's surprised by how sharp the branches are. He yelps as he's scratched the length of his forearm. He pulls his hands inside his sleeves and proceeds with his arms crossed in front of his face.

As soon has he's pushed past a branch, it springs back into place behind him, leaving no trace of his passage. He focuses on the grey stone of the archway that rises out of the bushes ahead and continues to force his way through. It doesn't take long, but he's panting and sweating by the time he gets there. *It's claustrophobic in here. Maybe the bushes won't be quite as dense closer to the Chasm? Only one way to find out.*

Using his newly developed technique of protecting his face, he continues to bush-bash his way towards the Chasm. After ten paces, he's still engulfed in greenery. He has a moment of panic that he's lost. But, checking behind him, there's the gateway, and beyond that, the pillar. *Whew.* He turns back and continues his battle with the foliage.

Suddenly, the bushes thin out and he stops, inches from a cliff plunging at his feet to depths unknown. He gasps, his heart hammering, taking in the view. He's heard people talking about 'the Chasm'. It's one thing to hear the word, but it's quite another to have it appear at your feet. It's deep and dark. And across the other side, there's land. His heart skips a beat. *Medar!* But it's so far across. He looks back at the archway.

"Line up the pillar and the gate."

He knows that voice. *The Ancient.* He needs to move to his right. He shuffles along, his back to the bushes and facing the Chasm. Checks behind him. Shuffles another five paces. Checks again. A few more ... *There's the stairway!* He blinks, but it's still there: hewn into the cliff, a staircase marches down, down, down into the Chasm.

Suddenly, he freezes. Someone's there, thrusting through the bushes, panting and grunting with exertion. He spins to face them. *Did they follow me?* Then he catches a pungent whiff. *Not a person!* He shoves his hand into his pocket, fumbling for his sling and stones. Slipping a stone into the sling, he starts spinning it, all the while scanning the shrubbery, aware of the fatal drop behind him. He shuffles forwards a few paces. *Where are you?*

Squealing, a wild boar breaks cover, charging straight for him. Aleryck lets the stone fly. and it smacks the animal between its eyes. *Shot!*

But his momentary triumph is instantly replaced with dismay as the boar keeps coming. Aleryck throws himself to the side, but it's not far enough. The air is knocked out of his lungs as the animal ploughs into him and they both tumble over the edge.

Thud!

Aleryck groans. Can't breathe. *Am I dead?* Pain washes over him. *I thought you weren't supposed to feel pain when you're dead. So maybe I'm not.* He's lying on his back. A hard ridge presses under his shoulders and one foot is stuck somehow, He cracks open his eyes and lifts his head. It's the boar. Aleryck's lying on the first stair and the boar is pinning his foot against the low wall that prevented him from toppling into the Chasm. *The boar!*

Suddenly alert, he strains to free his foot. *What if it revives?* His heart racing, he braces for purchase against the step and heaves. His foot pops free and Aleryck scrabbles back up the stairs, not taking his eyes off the creature. But it doesn't move. It's dead. *Thank the Ancient.* Sweat breaks out on his forehead, and he slumps forwards. *That was close.*

After a minute, his heartrate back to normal, he peers over the edge. It looks like ... *yes*, way down below is a bridge. He sucks in his breath. *Is it dangerous? Maybe.* He eyes up the dead boar a few steps below him and smiles. *But I can handle it.*

Chapter 12————————A DARING ATTEMPT

Taran doesn't know what wakes him, but suddenly, he's alert. Something's different. The campfire has burnt down to embers, and the air has a chill to it, telling him it's well past midnight. He strains his eyes. *There!* A figure is sneaking into the camp.

He wriggles to a sitting position. "Help us!" he hisses.

The figure freezes. Eyes glint as they look in his direction. The person creeps towards him. Their head flicks from one sleeping brother to the next.

Counting, perhaps?

"Why should I?" they whisper. "You left Aleryck to die."

Taran jerks upright. "How do you know Aleryck?"

The figure moves closer.

Taran realises with a start that it's a girl.

"You're Taran, right?" she asks.

Taran nods.

"I rescued Aleryck from the crevice you left him to die in."

Taran's heart leaps. Warmth floods him. "You ... Aleryck's alive?" he croaks.

"Yes—no thanks to you."

Taran breathes a silent prayer of thanks to the Ancient. "Did Aleryck send you to rescue us?" he whispers.

The girl makes a strange choking sound. "I'm here to help Aleryck. But not to rescue *you*. To rescue his tablet. Do you know where it is?"

"Yes, I do. I can help you get it!"

The girl goes completely still. "Like you helped Aleryck?"

A chill seeps into Taran's bones. He hangs his head. "I made a huge mistake," he says. "I'm so sorry. But if you free us, I promise I'll help you get the tablet."

The girl regards him. "How about, you tell me where the tablet is, and I'll think about freeing you," she says.

No! They have to get free. His brothers will never survive slavery. Especially not Seb, Kepler and Noor. Heck, even Baydar is too young. Tears threaten, and he brushes them away with his bound hands.

"Alright," he says. "I get it. I don't deserve to be freed. But this whole mess is my fault. The others only did what I told them to." He shrugs awkwardly at their sleeping forms beside him. "At least free them."

"Tell me where the tablet is," she repeats.

Taran jerks his head towards the largest of the tents. "It's in a chest inside that tent. I think the chest is locked."

The girl nods, then turns and creeps towards the tent, slipping silently inside.

Taran strains his ears, but he can't hear a thing.

The minutes drag.

Suddenly, a yell from Slasher splits the air. "Thief!" Three piercing whistles follow.

At the same instant, the girl sprints out of the tent, with Slasher hot on her heels. As she dashes past Taran, an object glints in the moonlight as it spins towards him. It lands with a thud, quivering at his feet. A knife. Frantically, he stretches out a foot and manages to scrape the blade towards him.

In a single fluid movement, the girl leaps onto one of the horses and gallops off into the night. She must've untethered it before he saw her. Perhaps that was what had woken him?

The camp explodes into life. Five Slavers dash past the trussed-up brothers, untether their horses and take off after the girl.

By now all his brothers are awake and wriggling into sitting positions. "What's going on?" Baydar asks, eyes wide.

Taran cranes his neck to look behind him. Several more Slavers are making for their horses, and within seconds they, too, join the pursuit.

The thud of hooves fades and, just like that, all is quiet again.

Taran clears his throat. "That," he says to his brothers, "was a girl stealing the tablet."

This announcement is followed by a barrage of questions, all asked at once.

"How do you know that?"

"Who is she?"

"How did she know to find it here?"

"How do you know she's a girl?"

"Why did she steal the tablet?"

"What's all this racket about, then?" asks someone. Not one of his brothers.

Taran curses. *Dog's dung, it's Cookie. I didn't realize he'd stayed behind.* "Ah, nothing sir. Just wondering what all the excitement's about."

Cookie scratches his head. "Not sure, really. All I know is something got stolen. Everyone's taken off after the thief, 'cept me left behind to guard you lot."

Taran thinks fast—this is their chance to escape! As Cookie turns away, Taran sweeps his bound legs at Cookie's feet, toppling the man to the ground.

Winded, Cookie lies there, groaning.

Taran aims a kick at the man's head and he goes still.

"What have you done?" Baydar asks. "Now what are we going to do?"

"I have a knife. Let me cut you free." He grins.

"What? Where did you get it?" Baydar asks, holding out his bound hands to Taran.

Taran has managed to grip the knife in his own bound hands, and awkwardly starts sawing the ropes around Baydar's wrists. "The girl threw it to us."

Baydar's eyebrows shoot up. "Why?"

"Hold still," Taran says. "I managed to talk to her before she stole the tablet. There, your hands are free. Now cut mine."

Baydar takes the knife and sets to Taran's bindings.

"She rescued Aleryck from the crevice and she was stealing the tablet to take it back to him."

Baydar stops cutting. "Aleryck's alive? Thank the Ancient!"

"Was Aleryck with her?" Seb asks.

Taran shakes his head. "No, just the girl. Anyhow, needless to say, Aleryck is pretty upset with us, and the girl said that she wasn't here to rescue us, just to get the tablet for Aleryck. Ah, that's better." He rubs his wrists as the ropes fall away. "Now free your feet, Baydar, then the others." He bends forward and starts working at the knot tying his own feet together.

Before long, they're all free.

"Now what?" Baydar asks.

Indeed, Taran's thoughts exactly. He'd led them wrong before, though. "What do you think, Baydar?" he asks.

"Me? I was thinking..."

Taran bites his tongue and nods encouragingly.

"... we should see if Aleryck needs help."

Noor, Seb and Kepler crowd around. "Yeah, let's go find Aleryck," Noor enthuses.

Taran slaps Baydar on the shoulder. "That's settled then. Have a quick search for some weapons and supplies and let's get out of here."

Minutes later they are jogging off in the direction the girl and her pursuers went, ready to dive into the bushes at any sign of the Slavers.

Chapter 13---------INTO MEDAR

Aleryck paces back and forth, back and forth, at the edge of the band of scrub. Juniper should be back by now. *Where is she?*

When she had gone scouting after they first arrived at the pillar, she returned within the hour to report that she'd found the Slaver camp not far away. Aleryck showed her the steps he'd discovered ... and the dead boar. Her eyes flashed, and she hugged him! His cheeks burn again just thinking about that hug.

"I'm impressed, Aleryck," she had said. "When it's well past midnight, I'll go steal your tablet back. There's a chance I'll get caught, but it's more likely I'll be chased. So, I'll need you to wait here for me—at the edge of the scrub—then I'll give you the tablet as I pass by. You melt into the bush and make your way into Medar via those secret steps. I'll throw the Slavers off my scent, then circle back to find you." She folded her arms across her chest. "Sound like a plan?"

He nodded, still feeling the pressure from her hug like a band around his chest. "Uh-huh," he managed.

They'd had a bite to eat and tried to get some sleep until it was time for Juniper to leave, but the various scenarios of how this could all go wrong tumbled about Aleryck's head like two-week-old puppies, and he couldn't settle. In the end they just talked quietly in the dark, not wanting to light a fire for fear of being seen. At one stage, Juniper asked him, "Aleryck, I saw your brothers all tied up together in the Slavers camp. If I get a chance, do you want me to free them?"

"No," he shot back. They'd left him down that crevice to die—so he'd leave them at the Slaver camp to die. But then his gut squirmed like a slippery eel. He hadn't died, had he? In fact, he'd been down that crevice for less than an hour before Juniper rescued him. And his brothers had been prisoners for weeks now. Maybe they, too, deserved a second chance.

"I dunno," he ventured eventually. "Perhaps. If it doesn't risk our task."

At last, it was time for her to go.

"Good luck, Juniper," he said.

"The Ancient is with us, Aleryck," she replied. "That's better than luck." Then she had disappeared into the dark night.

But that was over an hour ago. At least, it feels like it. Surely, she should be back by now? He chews a nail as he paces. Then, his head jerks up as galloping hoof beats approach. He strains his eyes. Could that be her? She didn't say anything about stealing a horse. What if it isn't? He half-crouches into the bushes in case he needs to hide.

"Aleryck!" she calls as she gallops past.

"Here," he shouts. An object flies over his head and lands in the bushes behind him.

He gropes his way into the scrub. *Where is it?* The wiry branches scratch at his face and arms as he flails about. *Did it land on a bush, or has it fallen to the ground?* He shakes the small tree nearest him. Then another. He drops to his knees and pats the ground, twigs catching in his hair. Dead leaves and sticks stab his palms. He pushes further into the bushes, shaking them and feeling the ground. A sob escapes him as he crawls forward, but then he freezes and holds his breath. The ground is vibrating. *Galloping goats!* No, he corrects himself. It's galloping horses.

"She went that way," a rough voice shouts.

It must be the Slavers. Hoping the bushes are thick enough to hide him, Aleryck manoeuvres around to a sitting position in the tight space. As he does so, his hand lands on something hard. Rectangular. Small—like a book. He scoops the tablet to his chest and closes his eyes. *Thank the Ancient.*

The ground stops shaking, and the hoof beats recede. He tucks the tablet into his satchel and cautiously stands, poking his head just above the top of the bushes. Can't see anyone, but there's the archway. He makes a beeline for it, but not too fast. He doesn't want to tumble into the Chasm ... again. He suddenly remembers Juniper's words, 'You melt into the bush.' He grins. Well, it was hardly 'melting', but he's got the tablet and has made it to the top of the stairs. Now for the hard part: climbing down in the dark. He hates descents. He takes a deep breath and shuffles his foot forward until he feels the edge of the stairs. He slides his good foot down to the first step, peering at the ground. It's so dark.

Suddenly, the moon breaks from behind a cloud, and the stairs are illuminated by a beam of pearly light. "Thank you," Aleryck breathes. Now at least he can see where to place his feet. With difficulty, he climbs over the boar. With one hand trailing the cliff face at his left and the other on the hip-height wall at his right, he slowly descends into the Chasm.

The steps are covered in moss and are crumbly. Every now and then his foot slides on the loose debris. But the wall—the only thing between him and a plunging drop into the Chasm—stops him from slipping too far.

He doesn't know how long it takes to reach the landing at the bottom of the staircase. It feels like hours, but it probably wasn't. His legs are shaking and his breathing ragged, so he sits on the bottom step to rest. In any event, there's still no sign of Juniper.

Sighing, Aleryck pushes himself upright. He needs to keep moving. He eyes up the bridge. It's narrow but has handrails. Luckily, the moonlight filters even this far down the Chasm. He shuffles out onto the structure, gripping the rails with both hands. Half-way across, a dank chill wafts up from the deep, ruffling his clothes and caressing his cheeks. He imagines the yawning Chasm dropping away beneath him and suddenly he can't move. He squeezes his eyes shut and concentrates on his breathing. A deep breath in ... and out. Calm settles over him. He opens his eyes and starts moving again.

Finally, the rails end, and he steps off the bridge onto a landing. He gazes up the vertical cliff in front of him. The sky has lightened, and, high above, the lip of the cliff is etched black against the grey dawn. Up there is Medar. He's nearly there.

He adjusts the satchel on his shoulder and starts the ascent. It's easier on his bad leg going up than it was coming down, especially as he's able to haul himself up using the wall. Every thirty steps or so, there's another landing, and the staircase changes direction, zigzagging up to the surface.

Finally, the top of the cliff draws near. He reaches up a hand and touches the grass hanging over the edge. *Medar.* He hurries up the final few steps and flops exhausted onto the dewy grass. He's made it.

After a few moments, he sits up, his feet dangling over the edge. He squints down into the Chasm, his eyes travelling across the bridge then up the staircase on the opposite side. Still no sign of Juniper.

Rolling to his feet he turns to see Medar. But all he can see is bushes: the same, wiry bushes that edged the Chasm on the Tyrelia side. Huffing, he sets to forcing his way through the scrub. After a few minutes he emerges onto a barren plain, dotted with grasses and thorny bushes. They stretch away, as far as he can make out in the dim dawn light. Nothing. There's nothing here.

His legs give way, and he drops to his knees. He's tired. So tired. Needs to rest. He crawls over to a large bush looming nearby and worms his way under the low-hanging branches. Unexpectedly, the ground slopes steeply down and, with a yelp, he starts rolling. Just as suddenly, he comes to a stop. His neck and legs are wedged up against something, but his middle sags, unsupported. He feels the ground around him with his hands. It's a tunnel! He wriggles around and faces the entrance, straining his ears. "Hello?" he says. "Is anyone there?"

Silence.

He crawls forwards, patting the earth before moving a knee. The tunnel is narrow, and his head brushes against roots that dangle through the roof. It's black as coal in here, so he senses rather than sees that the tunnel opens into a cave. He feels around and establishes that it's not much larger than he is. He can sit cross-legged, but not stand.

"Here."

Aleryck jumps with fright. It's been so long since he's heard the Ancient's voice, he isn't expecting it. "You mean, hide the tablet here, in this hole?"

"Yes."

He scrabbles away at the dirt in the floor of the cave. It's soft and easily dug, but the space is tight and he's sweating by the time he's done. He wraps the tablet in the goatskin and places it reverently in the hollow, then covers it up with the loose soil, packing it down.

He wipes a sleeve across his brow. "Now what?" he asks.

"Rest, Aleryck. You have done well."

That's a task he can certainly achieve. He curls against the dirt wall and in seconds he's asleep.

Chapter 14--------PURSUIT

Taran slows down. "Baydar," he calls in a low voice, "I don't know about you, but I can't tell if we're still going in the right direction."

Baydar steps close to Taran. "I agree. It's too dark to see any tracks. The only thing I can see is that pillar over there." He gestures to their right. It's a darker black finger stabbing into the ebony sky.

"Maybe we should hide there?" Taran says.

In response, Baydar leads the way. The brothers follow him in single file. As they reach its base, the moon emerges from behind a cloud and bathes them in silver light.

Taran whips his head around to check their surroundings, but there is nothing else moving as far as he can see. Still, they're too exposed. "Quick, around the back," he says.

As they huddle together behind the pillar, Noor leans into Taran and Baydar. "See that building over there?" he asks. "Shall I check if it's empty?"

Taran nods. "Good idea."

Noor scoots over to one corner of the building, then flattens himself against it. Sidling to a window, he peers in for a few heartbeats. Then, ducking under the sill, he creeps around the back and disappears. There's a faint rattling sound.

What is Noor doing? Taran purses his lips. Maybe he or Baydar should've gone. Noor's so clumsy, he'll probably wake whoever is inside. He drums his fingers on his thigh.

Before long, Noor runs back to join them. "It's empty," he says, "and the door's unlocked. I reckon we should stay there."

"Are you sure?" Taran asks.

"Yes, I'm sure." Noor plants his hands on his hips.

"Alright then, let's do it."

They dash over, following Noor around the side. Noor lets them in the door. It's a single room cabin without a stick of furniture. But it's dry, and there's a window facing out towards the Chasm: a perfect vantage point to spot the Slavers should they come past.

Taran claps Noor on the shoulder. "Good job, Noor," he says.

Baydar is staring out the window. "Hey," he says, "look at that."

"What is it?" Taran asks. He stands beside Baydar and peers out. It's an archway, like the one they saw near Beta the night the Slaver's took the tablet. "What's it doing there, do you think?"

Baydar shrugs. "No idea."

Taran turns, clapping his hands. "Right, we need to make a plan. I'm sure those Slavers will come back this way at some stage. We need to keep an eye out to see if they've caught that girl ... or worse, Aleryck. We'll need a rotating watch. One hour each. I'll go first. The rest of you try and get some sleep."

∞∞∞∞∞

Taran is woken by Baydar shaking his shoulder. He rouses instantly. "What is it?" he asks. *Baydar's watch.* He does the calculations in his head. It must be about five in the morning, then.

"Quick," Baydar says in a low voice. "Some of the Slavers just tracked something into the bushes."

The other brothers have roused. "Some? How many?" asks Noor.

"Five," says Baydar. "They were all there, about ten or twelve of them, on their horses. They were inspecting the ground, then five of them dismounted and went into the bushes, and the others, including Slasher, took their horses and headed back towards the camp."

Taran sucks in his breath. "So, we've got about fifteen minutes before they figure out that we're missing."

"Was Aleryck or the girl with them?" asks Kepler.

Baydar shakes his head. "No. That must be whose tracks they found. Come on, we've gotta go and follow those trackers. Now."

Seb and Kepler grab the weapons and dash out the door behind Baydar.

They race across the short distance to the archway, looming black against the grey dawn sky. Baydar points to some broken branches, directly in front of the archway. "They went in here."

Baydar enters first, then Taran, followed by Noor and Seb, with Kepler at the rear. It takes about ten paces, pushing their way through the dense bush, before they reach the structure. Taran glances up briefly as he passes underneath. *What's its purpose?* But another ten paces later, he stops abruptly as Baydar cries out, and his question is answered.

"Stairs!" Baydar exclaims in an excited whisper.

Taran holds his arms wide to prevent Noor, Seb and Kepler from stumbling over the cliff. "Shh," he hisses.

The brothers creep up beside him and Baydar gestures at the stairs. Their eyes go wide.

Taran crouches down, straining his ears. A scrabbling noise drifts up from below. *The Slavers.* He peers over the edge. *There's a bridge down there! Who knew?*

At the same time Baydar elbows him in the ribs, pointing across the Chasm. It's the girl, scrambling up the stairs on the other side, not too far from the top.

There's no time to lose. "She must know where Aleryck is," Taran whispers. "He's going to need our help. Let's go." He takes the lead down the stairs, his lips pressed into a straight line. *I won't let Aleryck down this time.*

Chapter 15--------DESTINY FULFILLED

"Aleryck!"

"Mmm?" Is his ma calling him to go tend the goats already? But he's still so tired. It can't be time to get up yet.

The voice calls again, "Aleryck. Where are you?"

His eyes pop open. That's not his ma's voice. He smells an earthy odour and feels dirt under his fingertips. That's right. He's in a cave, in Medar. And that's Juniper's voice, not Ma's.

He scrambles up the tunnel and emerges from under the bush into early dawn light. Juniper is silhouetted against the bushes a stone's throw away. "Juniper," he calls out. "I'm here."

"Aler—"

At that instant, five men leap from the bushes behind Juniper. One grabs her, holding her against his chest, pointing something at her throat.

A knife. It's a knife! Those men must be the Slavers. Hot anger consumes him. Without thinking, he dashes towards Juniper. "Let her go," he yells. His voice is high, like a child's.

A different man bursts out laughing, takes one stride towards Aleryck and scoops him up, pinning his arms to his sides. "And who do we have here?" he asks.

"Let me go!" Aleryck screams, thrashing his legs. His feet can't touch the ground, but he succeeds in kicking his captor in the shin.

"You little monkey," the man growls, dropping Aleryck and clasping his shin, rubbing it vigorously.

Aleryck scoots backwards, away from the man.

"Twotoes. Bundit. Get him, will you?" the man holding Juniper says. His voice sounds bored.

"Right you are, Bones." Twotoes and Bundit pounce on Aleryck and haul him to his feet, gripping his arms.

"You coming, Mouse?" Bones asks the one Aleryck kicked.

The man stops rubbing his shin and draws himself to his full height. He's a giant, not a mouse. He scowls at Aleryck, but replies, "Yeah, boss."

"That's better," Bones says. "Now, let's start again. Where is that tablet you stole from us?"

"Don't you mean that *you* stole from *us*?" says a voice from behind the Slavers.

"Taran!" Aleryck exclaims. Relief sweeps through his body, from his feet to his head, stretching him taller. He never thought he'd be so pleased to see his brother.

Now it's seven teenagers against five men. That's better odds.

Then it all happens at once. Noor swings a club hard at one of the men's legs, and he drops like a felled tree. At the same time, Baydar slashes a dagger across Mouse's back, and blood sprays out, splattering him. Mouse screams and falls to the ground, whilst Baydar dances backwards out of reach.

Twotoes and Bundit release Aleryck to face the attack, and Aleryck scrambles to the safety of a bush. Juniper uses the distraction to twist free, then shoves Bones hard. Bones stumbles backwards into Taran, who wrestles the dagger out of Bones' hand and flings it away. But Twotoes lunges, knocking Taran off their leader. They roll off, fists flying. All Aleryck can see is a tangle of limbs: legs kicking and arms shoving. Grunts and yells fill the air.

Suddenly, Bones' voice cuts through the din. "STOP," he roars. He has Baydar on his knees in front of him, a dagger to his throat.

Bundit holds a struggling Juniper.

Taran, astride Twotoes on the ground, stays the punch he is about to land.

Noor drops his club.

Seb is lying on the ground, apparently injured. Kepler is crouched over him, gently shaking his twin's shoulders, sobbing, "Seb, Seb, can you hear me?"

Two of the Slavers are out cold on the ground.

"Enough!" Bones shouts. "We can do this the hard way, or the easy way. The easy way is that one of you gives us that wretched tablet. The hard way is, well ..." He presses the tip of his dagger into Baydar's throat. A drop of red oozes at the point.

"Help me, Taran," Baydar croaks.

Aleryck's heart thumps. Taran *can't* help him. But Aleryck can. He's the only one who knows where the tablet is. He's the only one who can give it to the Slavers. But if he gives it to the Slavers, then what about his quest? What about all the people in Medar? And anyhow, if he gives the tablet to the Slavers, what's to say they won't kill them all anyway? Would they torture the tablet's hiding place out of him? He bites his lip. What should he do?

An idea slips into his head. It's a dark idea, black and venomous. *If I die, then the secret is safe. They will never discover where the tablet is hidden.*

He squeezes his eyes shut. *If only there was another way.* Even with his eyes closed, all he can see is that drop of blood on Baydar's throat. He opens his eyes and, as though in a trance, he stands up. Without meaning to, he says, "I have the tablet."

Bones' head snaps up. A smile spreads across his face.

Juniper gasps.

"Where is it?" Bones asks.

Aleryck gestures towards the Chasm. "I hid it over there," he lies, lifting his chin.

"Alright then," Bones says. "Go get it. And don't try anything funny. You know what will happen if you do." He smirks at Baydar and presses the blade harder into Baydar's throat.

Aleryck forces his legs to start walking towards the Chasm. He fixes his eyes on the strip of vegetation masking his destination. A cold numbness envelops his heart and starts seeping outwards, snaking down his arms and legs.

As he passes Juniper, she calls out, "No, Aleryck. Don't do it."

Does she know his intentions? He marches on. Passes Noor without acknowledging him. *Can't risk looking at him—might make me change my mind. Not far now. Then it will all be over.*

"Aleryck!"

The voice cuts through the fog in his mind, and he stops in his tracks. *Ancient?*

"What are you thinking? This is not my way! Ending your own life is never the answer," the Ancient says. The Ancient's voice is warm, unlike the other icy voice he heard. *Whose voice was that, then?*

"I have a better way. Do you trust me, Aleryck?"

∞∞∞∞∞∞

Taran flicks his gaze from Baydar to Aleryck. Aleryck hid the tablet in the Chasm? They must've walked straight past it. Aleryck looks very pale though. *Not like himself, really.* Taran turns his head to follow Aleryck's progress. *Nope, he looks positively wooden. What the …?*

Taran blinks and looks again. But Aleryck's not there. He has vanished.

∞∞∞∞∞∞

"Where did he go?" Bones demands.

Aleryck stares at Bones. Why is he saying that? He's right here. Isn't he? He looks down at himself. *Oh my.* He pats his chest. It's still there—but he's invisible!

At that moment, a shriek pierces the air and a dark shape plummets from the sky, talons out, and flies straight into Bones' head.

Bones screams. He flings his arms up to protect his face, dropping the dagger in the process.

Baydar throws himself to the side and rolls away.

Juniper, taking advantage of the moment, wrests herself from Bundit's grasp and sprints towards Aleryck. "Aleryck, where are you?"

She's going to miss him, though. He stumbles towards her, his arms outstretched. Grabs her sleeve and swings her off her trajectory.

They tumble to the ground. "Aleryck, is that you?" she asks when they stop rolling. "I can't see you."

Aleryck sucks in his breath and squeezes her hand. "I can't see you either, Juniper," he whispers. "You're invisible too. Quick, this way. Let's hide behind that bush."

"What bush?"

Of course, she can't see where he's pointing. He scrambles to his feet, never letting go of her hand, and tugs her to the bush. "The Ancient has made me invisible, and now you too, it would seem. But I'm not sure if you'll remain invisible if I let go of your hand. If we hide it won't matter if you become visible. Are you ready? I'm going to let go now." He loosens his grip.

"Are you still touching me?" Juniper asks.

Aleryck takes a step backwards, to make sure. Shakes his head. "No, I'm not. You're still invisible, Juniper."

"Now the girl has disappeared too," Bones yells. "Where did they go? Someone find them. Aargh!" he screams, throwing his arm up in front of his face as he fends off another attack from Aya.

"On it, boss," Bundit says. He races towards the spot where Juniper disappeared.

Juniper says, "I'll get the twins. You get another one of your brothers. Quick."

Aleryck hobbles off towards Noor, weaving around the man that Noor had knocked down with the club earlier, and who has finally regained his feet. The man takes a swing at Noor just as Aleryck barrels into Noor. Instantly Noor becomes invisible. "It's me, Aleryck," Aleryck whispers. "C'mon, let's go." He drags Noor away.

The Slaver stares bewildered at the now empty air in front of him. The blood drains out of his face and his mouth twists. "Ghosts!" he screams. He races off towards the Chasm. "Bundit, this place is haunted. Get out of here before they take us too." He pushes past Bundit and disappears back down the staircase into the Chasm. Bundit follows him without hesitation.

"Come back here, you cowards," Bones yells.

At that moment, both Baydar and Aya renew their attack on Bones. Baydar lands a solid punch to Bones' jaw, whilst Aya claws his face. Blood streams from a deep cut above his eye. Bones spins from the impact and lands heavily on the ground. Growling, he wipes his sleeve across his face before lurching back, arms outstretched, towards Baydar. Who is suddenly no longer there. Bones sprawls face down onto the dirt. Rolling quickly to his feet, he stands with his fists clenched, his head whipping around. "Stop it!" he yells, spit flying from his mouth. "Stop disappearing." His gaze fastens on Taran, who is once again sitting astride Twotoes, pinning him to the ground.

Twotoes lets out a yelp and shoves Taran off him. Mumbling something incoherent, Twotoes dashes off towards the Chasm and disappears over the edge.

Taran scrambles to his feet, looking around. Mouse is still lying on the ground when Baydar slashed him at the start. Taran lifts a shoulder and smirks. "Looks like it's just you and me now, Bones," he says. And promptly turns invisible.

Bones stares for a second at the spot where Taran disappeared, before lunging towards it with a roar. He swings a punch, but his blow doesn't connect. He swings again but misses once more.

"Cowards! You're all cowards," he screams, before turning on his heel. Dragging Mouse to his feet, they stumble back to the Chasm and down the stairs.

Aleryck creeps after him and watches until he's sure they're not coming back.

Chapter 16--------A NEW TASK

"He's the one who's acting like a coward," Aleryck says. And with those words, he becomes visible.

One by one, like fireflies blinking into existence at dusk, Juniper, Taran, Baydar, Noor, Kepler and Seb all appear. Juniper is crouched over by Seb and Kepler, both sitting on the ground. Aya swoops down and settles on her shoulder. Noor is off to her left, and Baydar and Taran stand not too far from where they outwitted their Slaver opponents.

Taran turns to Aleryck, a look of incredulity on his face. "What was that, Aleryck?"

Noor rushes over and slings his arm around Aleryck, almost knocking him off balance. "Whatever it was, it was *amazing*," he exclaims.

Aleryck beams around at them all and shrugs his shoulders. "I don't know what it was, Taran. But I know who did it. It was the Ancient."

Taran nods his head slowly. "Did you know the Ancient was going to turn us all invisible?"

A dull heat floods Aleryck's cheeks. He studies his feet. "Uh, no. I ..." He can't bring himself to tell them what he had been planning to do. What he had thought was the answer to getting them out of this predicament. *Killing myself.*

Juniper stands and walks over to Aleryck. "Thank the Ancient," she says. "But thank you too, Aleryck. Without your quick thinking we might not have got all of us turned invisible in time." She steps up to Taran and holds out her hand. "I'm Juniper, by the way. We didn't manage to introduce ourselves properly last time."

Taran laughs, shaking her hand. "No, we certainly did not. I'm Taran."

"Hang on a minute," Aleryck says. "Did you make Baydar invisible, Juniper?"

"Is that one of the twins?" Juniper asks. "If so, yes, I did."

"No," Aleryck says. "Of course, you don't know who everyone is. Let me introduce you." He rattles off his brothers' names, pointing at each one in turn.

Juniper shakes her head, looking at Baydar. "No, I thought you must've, Aleryck. I stayed over there with the twins."

"And I helped Noor," Aleryck adds, "but everything happened so fast after that, I was busy trying to not get trampled."

"So, what you're saying," Baydar says slowly, "is that the Ancient himself made Taran and me invisible? Awesome. Does that make us as special as you, Aleryck?"

At the mention of the word 'special', Aleryck remembers how proud he was that the Ancient had chosen him to inscribe the tablet and bring it to Medar. But he has no right to that pride. He didn't achieve this task single-handed! Without Juniper's help, he would never have known how to get into Medar. And if Taran and his brothers hadn't abandoned him in the Wastelands, he would never have met Juniper. Could the Ancient have allowed his brothers to steal the tablet? Was it possible that the Slavers taking his brothers captive was all part of some great plan? He should never have doubted the Ancient. Never. And he almost spoiled the Ancient's perfect plan by trying to take his own life.

The shame of it all suddenly engulfs Aleryck, and he sinks to the ground.

Taran dashes to him, catching him before he falls. "Aleryck, are you alright?"

Aleryck nods, blinking back tears. "I'm so sorry," he whispers.

Taran frowns. "You're sorry?" he asks. "What in the name of the Ancient for? It's me who needs to apologise, Aleryck. I … I was awful to you. I guess … I was jealous." It comes out in a rush.

Aleryck lifts his chin. "You were jealous of me?" he asks. His lips form a crooked smile. "That's got to be a first."

"I know, right? But you know what?" Taran squeezes Aleryck's shoulders. "You were amazing. I'm so proud of you."

Baydar crouches down beside them, placing a strong hand on each of their shoulders. "I'm proud of you too, Aleryck. I'm proud of all of us."

Noor throws himself on to the group, knocking them all over, exclaiming, "Me too!"

Kepler rushes over. "Dog pile!" he yells, jumping onto his brothers.

"Woo hoo," Seb adds, fist-pumping the air, but remaining seated on the ground.

Juniper stands, hands on hips, shaking her head at the giggling, groaning pile of brothers. "I'm so glad I'm not a boy," she says.

Aleryck rolls out from the tangle of bodies. It's as if a weight has been lifted off him. And it's not his brothers.

The others slowly untangle themselves and form a rough circle, seated on the ground. Juniper joins them. "Now what?" she asks, looking from one to the other.

"Aleryck, is the tablet safe?" Taran asks.

Aleryck nods. "Yes, it is."

"So, the task's accomplished, then?" Juniper asks.

"Yes and no," whispers the Ancient into Aleryck's mind.

Aleryck's head snaps up. "What do you mean?"

"Huh?" Juniper says.

Aleryck holds his hand up, palm towards her. "I'm not talking to you," he says. He closes his eyes and opens his mind. *What do you mean, Ancient?*

"Yes, you have done as I asked with regards to the tablet. But now I have a new task for you, Juniper, and your brothers. Do you remember when we first met, I told you that my people here in Medar are lost?"

Yes, but I don't understand what that means.

"What you have done for me was unselfish, Aleryck. What I asked of you, wasn't easy. And yet you chose to do it."

And I'm so glad I did! I've discovered that I can do so much more than I thought. I met Juniper. And now Taran and I are friends again. None of that would've happened if I hadn't chosen to accept your task.

"Don't you think everybody should be given a chance to grow and learn, like you did? By doing something for a cause that is bigger than themselves? How will they do that if they don't know my voice?"

But you're all-powerful. Couldn't you force them to listen to you?

"Ah, Aleryck. That is not my way. Whilst I know that my ways are best, I want people to choose to follow them. Freely. But with free choice comes a risk."

What risk?

"The risk that they won't choose to follow my ways. That they will make choices that hurt others and themselves. But if they don't know my ways, then those are the only choices they will be able to make."

What can we do?

"A time will come when Medar will need my gifts of invisibility and warping. Will you help teach others how to wield these gifts? Will you and your brothers and Juniper take on this new task?"

But I don't know how it all works—either the warping or the invisibility, Aleryck protests.

"I will teach you all. If you're willing."

Aleryck opens his eyes. His brothers and Juniper are all staring at him.

"Well?" Taran asks. "What is the Ancient saying to you?"

Aleryck smiles around at them. "You mean, what is the Ancient saying to all of us?" he says.

"Really?" Noor asks. "Even me?"

Aleryck grins, nodding. "Yes, even you, Noor." Aleryck catches their gaze, one by one, as he says, "The Ancient wants to know if we will all, including you, Juniper, teach others how to become invisible and to how to warp."

Taran grips Aleryck's shoulder, grinning. "I don't know what warping is, but I trust you, Aleryck. If the Ancient is asking us to do this, then yes, I'm in."

Baydar nods. "Yes, of course, Aleryck. Me too."

"Yes," says Juniper.

"Yes from me," adds Noor.

"Yes!" exclaim the twins together.

"That's settled, then," Aleryck says.

"We should seal it with an oath," Juniper suggests. "That's how my clan would do it, anyhow."

"That's a good idea," Aleryck says. "Can you lead it? I wouldn't have a clue ..."

Juniper nods. "Of course. All hold hands. Good. Now, repeat after me: We the—" She stops.

"What's wrong?" Taran asks.

"We need a name. For our group," says Juniper.

"Adelphi," says the Ancient into Aleryck's mind.

"Adelphi," Aleryck blurts.

"Oh, that's perfect," Juniper says.

"It is?" Aleryck asks. "What does it mean?"

Juniper raises an eyebrow at him. "You suggested it."

Aleryck shakes his head.

"Oh," Juniper says. "Well, it means 'brothers'. Where were we? That's right. We the Adelphi ..."

"We the Adelphi ..."

"Do solemnly swear to serve the Ancient," Juniper says.

"Do solemnly swear to serve the Ancient," the brothers repeat.

"To teach his ways to all those who are willing, from this day forth."

"To teach his ways to all those who are willing, from this day forth."

"And to always do what Juniper asks."

"I'm not agreeing to that!" Taran says, yanking his hand out of hers.

Juniper bursts out laughing and punches him lightly on his arm. "I'm joking."

"Are you allowed to joke during a serious ceremony?" Seb asks.

Juniper flicks her heavy braid over her shoulder. "Yes, you are. And besides, the ceremony is over."

The brothers release hands. "Now what?" Baydar asks.

Noor's stomach growls loudly, and he clutches it, a look of embarrassment on his face.

"Now," Taran says, "we should get something to eat." He winks at Noor. "And then we'll go home."

"Home," Aleryck says. "I like the sound of that."

EPILOGUE

It has been another hard day, practicing warping at the new school of the Adelphi—if you can call it that. In reality, it's just Aleryck and his brothers hanging out with Juniper and her clan.

This is too hard, Aleryck complains.

"Take heart. It will all be worth it. Remember, one day, the tablet will be found, and these skills will be necessary to save the one who discovers the tablet," says the Ancient.

I forgot to ask. When will that be?

"In a thousand years."

Aleryck gulps. A thousand years? That's a long time. He hopes the Adelphi will remain faithful until then. But of course, what's the point of faith unless there's something to believe in? Thankfully, they have something mighty to believe in: The Ancient.

THE END ... AND JUST THE BEGINNING

DEAR READER

I hope you enjoyed reading my book as much as I enjoyed writing it. If you would like to, I'd really appreciate it if you could write a review of *The Tablet*. Reviews make such a difference to other readers helping them to determine if they'd like to read a book or not. So, you, the reader, have the power to make or break a book. If you have time, please leave a review on Amazon:

www.amazon.com/author/srmanssen[1] Just type the link into your browser, click on the book then scroll down to the Customer Reviews section. Click on the button "Write a customer review" and you'll be taken to a page where you can leave your thoughts.

You can write to me at **realmtrilogy@gmail.com**, or follow me on these social media platforms:

Website:

http://www.srmanssen.com

Facebook:

https://www.facebook.com/realmtrilogy/

Smashwords:

https://www.smashwords.com/profile/view/SharonManssen

LinkedIn:

https://www.linkedin.com/in/sharon-manssen/

---

1.   http://www.amazon.com/author/srmanssen

ACKNOWLEDGEMENTS

Being the fourth book I've written, I somehow thought it would be easier than the others. It wasn't. I still had to squeeze writing around work and life commitments. So once again, I must thank my number one supporter and encourager: my husband, Craig. Thank you for your patience and endless support on this journey—especially for being my Alpha reader and critic.

Joining Tauranga Writers was a pivotal moment in my writing journey: I've been inspired and helped by many authors who are now friends, and I have learned so much about everything from the craft of writing to how to produce a publishable work.

Thank you to Chad Dick who gave so generously of his expertise whilst editing my manuscript, and to my beta readers: Brenda, Karen, Lee, Gerardine and Tracy—but especially my nephews Max and George. The story would not be nearly as good without all of your inputs.

Sharon Manssen
March 2023

ABOUT THE AUTHOR

A fantasy fan since being read 'The Hobbit' by her father at the fireside at the age of six, she has been an avid bookworm her entire life. When the idea for her current trilogy popped into her head, there was never any doubt that it would be in the fantasy genre. Unfortunately, real life gets in the way, and writing has to fit around her full-time job at a global engineering consultancy and family life (husband and two young adult children). It took ten years to pen her first book, Medar, which was a finalist for the Tom Fitzgibbon Award in 2015 and was published in 2017. Her second book, Tyrelia (2019) was a finalist in the Young Adult Fiction category in the 2020 Sir Julius Vogel Awards. Her third book, Golden City (2020), was a finalist in the Young Adult Fiction caterogy in the 2021 Sir Julius Vogel Awards and also in the 2021 Young Adult fiction category for the Caleb Awards.

MEDAR – realmshift trilogy book ONE

Sneak preview

Chapter 1---------Freya

Freya's heart pounded as she sprinted through the scrub. Her sandals scattered tiny stones with each footfall, her honey-brown braids slapped her back and her long fringe fell into her eyes. Another rock whizzed by her head as she finally made it into the darkness of the shadow of the Wall. Due to the lateness of the day the shadow cast a great distance, making it difficult for her pursuers to see her. She ducked and dodged between the scraggy mass of thorny bushes that grew close to the edge of the Chasm.

In this part of Medar the combination of poor soils and proximity to the Wall meant that nothing grew well, but this close to the Chasm the vegetation consisted entirely of tussock grasses and stunted plants, interspersed with scraggly pine trees.

Freya skidded under a particularly dense bush into a well-concealed hiding place. Her homespun leggings and leather tunic protected her from the thorny spikes above and the rough gravelly surface she was now lying on. This was familiar territory for her, and she knew that they wouldn't follow her here. Most people didn't dare come this close to the edge of the Chasm: a vertical drop to the depths of the land. But Freya had been here many times before and she was sure-footed and confident of her location.

She lay absolutely still, slowed her breathing, and listened for her pursuers. They moved through the bushes, only half-heartedly searching now, and their voices were uncertain as they approached the shadow. She concentrated on making as little noise as possible. They were just some of the village boys, a few years older than her, chasing her for sport. She was used to it; at nearly fourteen years old, she had never had any friends, due to her deformity. Her mother told her it had happened when she was about nine months old and was just learning to crawl.

Her mother, Martha, had been doing the weekly clothes wash. It was a laborious and sweaty job, plunging the clothing in the pot full of water, boiling above the hearth. She would use a stick to scoop the steaming clothes out of the pot and swing them at arms' length into the scrubbing tub. Martha said she could've sworn Freya was sitting in the far corner of the room, playing with pine cones and yet, somehow, as she swung the streaming clothes from the boiling water, there was Freya pulling herself up by the edge of the tub. She'd had no time to stop the motion and had struck the baby fully on the left side of her face with the scalding clothes.

Martha had immediately dropped the clothes and rushed the screaming Freya to the nearest cold water, which happened to be in a bucket beside the door. She couldn't immerse the scalded area under water for fear of drowning her, so she'd splashed handfuls of water onto the baby's face as best she could, at the same time trying to console the screaming infant who writhed in her grip. It was lucky she had been able to cool the area so quickly, for although the skin was terribly blistered, it did heal and eventually faded to almost the same shade as the rest of her skin. But her left eye could not be saved: the iris had turned a milky green and the eyelid drooped, causing it to appear half shut. It had not taken long to realise that the child had lost all sight from the eye.

Despite the loss of one eye, Freya had grown normally in every other respect, and her mother had encouraged her to leave her fringe long, to conceal the abnormal eye as best she could. Nevertheless, it had been the source of much teasing and ridicule from the other children in the village. From a young age, Freya had learned to avoid them as much as possible and was quite content roaming around by herself.

When she was old enough, her parents gave her responsibility for looking after their goat, Nan. She got up early each morning to milk her. The warm liquid was delicious on their gruel, but barely enough for a family of four. Her older brother, Jack, was already seventeen and helped her parents to tend their crops—he had no time for his annoying younger sister. After she had completed her morning chores, Freya would release the goat out to the scrublands to graze at will on the sparse, tough grasses that grew at the village outskirts. Then it was off to school for the morning. She liked learning, but as none of the other children wanted to play with her, it was hardly a time she enjoyed. After lunch at home with her mother, and some quick chores, she was free to do as she liked, as long as she kept watch over the goat and herded it each evening into the lean-to adjacent to their home.

And so, Freya had become accustomed to solitude and, with the freedom to wander far and wide, she had explored the scrublands. At the village outskirts were the fields where the farmers grew their meagre crops. Beyond the fields, scruffy grasses grew in the poor soils, with gnarled, scrawny bushes dotted irregularly over the landscape—except for behind the village, to the west. In that direction, the bushes and scrub became thicker and denser, for in that direction lay the Chasm, and few people had any reason to go there.

As its name suggested, the Chasm was a rift in the earth that varied from less than one to more than five kilometres wide. It encircled the whole land of Medar, so that it was like an island. The Chasm was impossibly deep and, with nearly vertical sides, nobody ventured close to the edge—nobody who valued their life, anyhow. Once she'd thrown a rock the size of her fist over the edge—lobbed it as far into the Chasm as she could—and she'd never heard it hit anything, even though she'd strained her ears for a full ten minutes.

Beyond the Chasm was the Wall.

The grey mass of the Wall rose vertically from the top of the cliff on the opposite side of the Chasm until it disappeared into a pall of dirty, grey clouds. It was said that it never ended. Freya knew from stories that the Wall encircled the whole Land and that it was impenetrable. The Wall was always there and had always been a part of their lives. Its shadow reduced the sunlight available and this, in addition to living in a part of the Land that was less fertile than most, often meant that their crops were poor. What they did grow was barely enough to keep the family fed, and they hardly had any left to trade for other items they might need. Freya had never thought too much about the Wall. It was just a fact of life, like rain and clouds and the Master.

The boys weren't giving up this time, and Freya could hear them getting closer to her hiding place. Carefully, silently, she withdrew deeper into the depths of the thorny bush. Suddenly she froze and gasped as she realised that her feet were no longer resting on the ground but were dangling in mid-air! Luckily, the sound of her gasp was drowned out for, at that very moment, there was a thunder of galloping hooves.

One of the boys shouted, "Guards!"

"Quick, let's go!" yelled another.

The apprehension was clear in their voices, as they raced off, back towards the safety of the village, their prey instantly forgotten. For just as everyone knew to stay away from the Chasm, so too they knew to steer clear of the Guards.

The Guards' sole purpose was to conduct the Master's business, and the Master's business was to prosper from Medar. When it came to the Guards, it was best to keep a low profile and draw as little attention to oneself as possible. There were rumours that bad things happened to people who got in the way of them.

Freya held her breath as the beating hooves came closer and closer ... but did not slow, and raced by. The sound faded into the distance. She breathed a sigh of relief and drew her legs quickly towards her stomach. How could she be so close to the Chasm? She must've lost her bearings. But no, she saw as she craned her neck under her arm, it wasn't the edge of the Chasm at all. She manoeuvred herself around under the bush, ducking her head so that she could have a better look, her hair catching in the thorns.

The bush's gnarled roots clung to the edge of a hole in the ground—perhaps an old well. The opening was not large, but more than big enough for Freya to fall in. She wormed her way closer so she could peer in with her good eye. No, it wasn't a well after all, as it was not a vertical shaft. Rather the walls of the hole sloped downwards at a gentle gradient, so that this was more like a tunnel than a hole.

The fading light meant that she could not see much at all. Curious, she reached for the tinder-box in her old leather satchel. She always carried that, slung diagonally over her shoulder, and it was now resting on her back. Gathering a small pile of twigs at the lip of the hole, she struck a spark onto the dry tinder and dropped it into the kindling. Instantly, the twigs crackled with flame. Taking care not to prick herself on the thorns, she snapped a thicker branch off the bush and held it to the fire. As soon as the branch caught, she threw a handful of dirt on the pile to extinguish the last flames, then carefully poked her burning stick into the void.

Her makeshift torch did not cast its light very far, but it was enough to see that the tunnel continued to angle downwards. She slithered into the hole and wriggled carefully forwards on her belly and elbows, shielding the flame with her hand. The cavity was not large and ended a few metres farther down in an enlarged, dug out space—a cave! Freya could fit all the way in and sit down with only a small clearance above her head. If she had been much bigger, she would not even have been able to manoeuvre herself around. Whoever had made this place couldn't have been much bigger than her.

The feathery roots of the bush grew through the ceiling of the cave and brushed her head. It smelt earthy, but it was dry. Careful not to touch the flame to the roots, Freya shone her torch around the confined space. The flame flickered and her shadow danced over the walls and ceiling. But the fading daylight was still visible at the entrance of the tunnel, and her torch was not in danger of going out. What a great little hiding place! She would turn it into a proper hidey-hole, her own secret place. Yes, she would come back tomorrow and bring some candles. Maybe she could even sneak one of her mother's old blankets? She grinned, delighted with her discovery.

As she wriggled around to crawl back out of the tunnel, her foot caught in something on the floor of the cave. She tugged her ankle, but it wouldn't come loose. Carefully, she reached back under herself to free the obstruction, expecting to feel a plant root. Instead, her hand encountered leather—there was something buried in the floor of the cave! Holding her breath, she scraped away the dirt with one hand, the other holding her burning stick.

Her excavation revealed a leather-wrapped object about the size of a small book. She prised it out of the ground and unwrapped it: it was some sort of tablet, and glinted and shone in the light. It seemed to be made of glass, but the surface was cloudy. It was hard to tell what it was in this light. It looked like it should be heavy, but she was surprised to feel it weighed hardly anything. And then, as she held her flame close to the object to examine it more carefully, she gasped as writing appeared on the surface, faint at first, then clear and bright:

Tyrelia! Land of gold
A land so lovely to behold
0, land of beauty, land of light
Joyous refuge, pure delight
Tyrelia! That land so fair
Of meadows green and clean pure air
Of stately trees in forests vast
Of ancient rocks from ages past

Then she noticed, etched into the bottom of the tablet, the following numbers: 50 - 63 - 92 - 99

Suddenly, she coughed as the smoke from her torch, which had been building up in the small space, caught in her throat. Hastily, she extinguished her flame and, more by feel than sight, she wrapped the leather back around the tablet, stuffed it into her satchel, and crawled back up the tunnel. Having wormed back out from under the bush, her heart thumping with excitement as much as exertion, she realised with alarm that it was almost dark—she should have been home ages ago. Sure that her mother would be worried, she quickly surveyed the scrub so she could memorise the location, and noted a large boulder a stone's throw away. With a satisfied nod, Freya turned on her heel and set off for the village at a jog, calling to Nan as she went. It was not long before she heard the clanking of the goat's bell. As she herded it before her, she pondered her strange discovery. She couldn't wait to get home and look at it again.

As she neared her hut, a murmur of voices reached her ears and her thoughts immediately jumped to the thundering horsemen. She'd forgotten all about them. Rounding a bend in the path, a dozen people came into view, crowded around the doorway to her home. Immediately thinking something bad must have happened, she tied

Nan back in her lean-to, and ran to the front of the house. But as she got closer she saw that the people were laughing and chatting happily, not in distress at all. Relieved, she squeezed her way through the throng and into her home. Her mother was busy chattering away to two other women and hadn't noticed her enter.

She tugged on her mother's sleeve. "What's happened, Ma? I heard the horsemen ..."

Her mother looked down at her with a flushed face and wide smile, her eyes sparkling. "Oh, Freya, there you are! We've been looking everywhere for you. You'll never believe it ... I can hardly believe it myself. Oh, it's our lucky day!"

Martha swept Freya into her arms and spun her around.

"Ma, calm down. You're not making any sense!" Freya laughed as Martha put her down, the jovial atmosphere contagious. "What's happened?"

Her mother cupped Freya's face with both hands and announced in a breathless voice, "We've been Selected!"

Stunned, Freya stood motionless for a second, then jabbed her fist into the air and whooped with delight.

Her father and brother came over, and her father gathered the whole family into a massive bear hug, tears of happiness streaming down his face.

"That's right, Freya," he laughed. "Golden City, here we come.

PURCHASE MEDAR **https://books2read.com/u/3RLZzx**
Purchase Tyrelia **https://books2read.com/u/38P1MV**
Purchase   Golden   City   **https://www.bklnk.com/**
B0BTBG6ML6